RUN
TO ME

By the Author

Love on Location

Run to Me

What Reviewers Say About Bold Strokes Books

"With its expected unexpected twists, vivid characters and healthy dose of humor, *Blind Curves* is a very fun read that will keep you guessing." – *Bay Windows*

"In a succinct film style narrative, with scenes that move, a character-driven plot, and crisp dialogue worthy of a screenplay ... the Richfield and Rivers novels are ... an engaging Hollywood mystery ... series." – *Midwest Book Review*

Force of Nature "...is filled with nonstop, fast paced action. Tornadoes, raging fire blazes, heroic and daring rescues... Baldwin does a fine job of describing the fast-paced scenes and inspiring the reader to keep on turning the pages." – *L-word.comLiterature*

In the Jude Devine mystery series the "...characters seem fully capable of walking away from the particulars of whodunit and engaging the reader in other aspects of their lives." – *Lambda Book Report*

Mine "...weaves a tale of yearning, love, lust, and conflict resolution ... a believable plot, with strong characters in a charming setting." – *JustAboutWrite*

"While these two women struggle with their issues, there is some very, very hot sex. If you enjoy complex characters and passionate sex scenes, you'll love *Wild Abandon*." – *MegaScene*

"*Course of Action* is a romance ... populated with a host of captivating and amiable characters. The glimpses into the lifestyles of the rich and beautiful people are rather like guilty pleasures ... a most satisfying and entertaining reading experience." – *Midwest Book Review*

The Clinic is "...a spellbinding novel." – *JustAboutWrite*

"*Unexpected Sparks* lived up to its promise and was thoroughly enjoyable ... Dartt did a lovely job at building the relationship between Kate and Nikki." – *Lambda Book Report*

"*Sequestered Hearts* ... is everything a romance should be. It is teeming with longing, heartbreak, and of course, love. As pure romances go, it is one of the best in print today." – *L-word.comLiterature*

"*The Exile and the Sorcerer* is a mesmerizing read, a tour-de-force packed with adventure, ordeals, complex twists and turns, and the internal introspection of appealing characters." – *Midwest Book Review*

The Spanish Pearl is "...both science fiction and romance in this adventurous tale ... A most entertaining read, with a sequel already in the works. Hot, hot, hot!" – *Minnesota Literature*

"A deliciously sexy thriller … *Dark Valentine* is funny, scary, and very realistic. The story is tightly written and keeps the reader gripped to the exciting end." – *JustAbout Write*

"*Punk Like Me* … is different. It is engaging. It is life-affirming. Frankly, it is genius. This is a rare book in that it has a soul; one that is laid bare for all to see." – *JustAboutWrite*

"*Chance* is not a novel about the music industry; it is about a woman discovering herself as she muddles through all the trappings of fame." – *Midwest Book Review*

Sweet Creek "… is sublimely in tune with the times." – *Q-Syndicate*

"*Forever Found* … neatly combines hot sex scenes, humor, engaging characters, and an exciting story." – *MegaScene*

Shield of Justice is a "…well-plotted…lovely romance…I couldn't turn the pages fast enough!" – Ann Bannon, author of *The Beebo Brinker Chronicles*

The 100th Generation is "…filled with ancient myths, Egyptian gods and goddesses, legends, and, most wonderfully, it contains the lesbian equivalent of Indiana Jones living and working in modern Egypt." – *Just About Write*

Sword of the Guardian is "…a terrific adventure, coming of age story, a romance, and tale of courtly intrigue, attempted assassination, and gender confusion … a rollicking fun book and a must-read for those who enjoy courtly light fantasy in a medieval-seeming time." – *Midwest Book Review*

"*Of Drag Kings and the Wheel of Fate*'s lush rush of a romance incorporates reincarnation, a grounded transman and his peppy daughter, and the dark moods of a troubled witch—wonderful homage to Leslie Feinberg's classic gender-bending novel, *Stone Butch Blues*." – *Q-Syndicate*

In *Running with the Wind* "…the discussions of the nature of sex, love, power, and sexuality are insightful and represent a welcome voice from the view of late-20-something characters today." – *Midwest Book Review*

"Rich in character portrayal, *The Devil Inside* is an unusual, unpredictable, and thought-provoking love story that will have the reader questioning the definition of right and wrong long after she finishes the book." – *JustAboutWrite*

Wall of Silence "…is perfectly plotted and has a very real voice and consistently accurate tone, which is not always the case with lesbian mysteries." – *Midwest Book Review*

RUN
TO ME

by

Lisa Girolami

2008

RUN TO ME
© 2008 BY LISA GIROLAMI. ALL RIGHTS RESERVED.

ISBN 10: 1-60282-034-1
ISBN 13: 978-1-60282-034-0

THIS TRADE PAPERBACK ORIGINAL IS PUBLISHED BY
BOLD STROKES BOOKS, INC.
NEW YORK, USA

FIRST EDITION: OCTOBER 2008

THIS IS A WORK OF FICTION. NAMES, CHARACTERS, PLACES, AND
INCIDENTS ARE THE PRODUCT OF THE AUTHOR'S IMAGINATION OR
ARE USED FICTITIOUSLY. ANY RESEMBLANCE TO ACTUAL PERSONS,
LIVING OR DEAD, BUSINESS ESTABLISHMENTS, EVENTS, OR LOCALES
IS ENTIRELY COINCIDENTAL.

THIS BOOK, OR PARTS THEREOF, MAY NOT BE REPRODUCED IN ANY
FORM WITHOUT PERMISSION.

CREDITS
EDITOR: JENNIFER KNIGHT
PRODUCTION DESIGN: STACIA SEAMAN
COVER DESIGN BY SHERI (GRAPHICARTIST2020@HOTMAIL.COM)

Acknowledgments

I have much respect and admiration for Len Barot. Thank you for adopting me.

Jennifer Knight, you are an incredible editor and I am in awe of you.

Stacia, thank you for pulling the details of this story into a tight piece.

Sheri, I love the cover design. Thank you!

To Lauren, who was the grist for this mill.

Lori (Andy), you are always there to reach out and help. You are so cool.

Warm hugs to the entire BSB family for your consistent and generous support.

Thank you to all the BSB readers who are a most amazing group of magnificent people.

And a special acknowledgment to the City by the Bay, San Francisco.

Dedication

To my mom, Kris, whom I lost a week before the publication
of *Love on Location*. She was so proud of me, and I wish
she had been able to hold my first novel in her hands.
She is forever in my heart.

It's an odd thing, but anyone who disappears is said to be seen in San Francisco.

—Oscar Wilde

CHAPTER ONE

Beth Standish braced herself against the icy wind that slapped her cheeks. As she stood alone in a pool of light at the all-night gas station, frigid gusts snapped up the back of her jacket. She rocked in time to the click-click of the gasoline pump, mostly to stay warm, but also in a feeble attempt to cajole the gas into her tank faster. The attendant, who had said nothing when she passed three twenty dollar bills through the tray, sat in his bulletproof enclosure staring blankly her way.

She looked south, in the direction she'd just come, then turned her gaze to the mountains that represented the dividing line between L.A. and the expanse of Central and Northern California. Staring up at the black peaks, she wondered if she would ever feel better, or if, perhaps, the shifts she felt within were permanent, like erosion—the alteration of her inner landscape by external forces. Maybe she would never get back to being herself, because that woman no longer existed.

With a sharp sigh, she capped the gas tank and got back in her car. She still had a four-hour drive ahead of her, but her journey was more complicated than mere geography. She had tried to frame it in her mind as an adventure, rich with possibilities, but she still felt like she was simply running away. Her race number and directions to the San Francisco Half Marathon were tucked neatly inside an envelope on the passenger seat next to her. She was looking forward to the challenge of a long and difficult race, but she had much more painful reasons for leaving Los Angeles. The race was just an excuse.

"God damn, Stephanie," she muttered, wishing she sounded angry instead of wistful and broken.

Pushing those excruciating, ever-present thoughts out of her head, she started the car and rejoined Interstate 5 north. The dark miles rolled endlessly on, with the sky as black as the road, and the horizon imperceptible in between. By the time the clock in the dash of her Mercedes 280 coupe ticked past three a.m., she was well north of Bakersfield. Over two hundred miles stretched ahead, broken by an occasional faded billboard or tired farm-road sign. The straight road in front of her seemed to swim. Beth blinked as the road seemed to wash into a clean black screen on which images of the last few months played over and over. Through her windshield it was as if she could see some kind of warped, late-night rerun in which she was the star.

"You're so fucking perfect," Stephanie screamed at her.

"I don't need you to be facetious, Steph."

"Don't think for a minute I don't mean it."

"This conversation isn't going anywhere."

Stephanie's expression was cynical. "Yeah, just like our relationship."

Beth's chest hurt. She could still feel the tension crushing her as the most painful events ran and reran, the voices screaming in her ears. Late-night arguments, public scenes, bitter looks. The shock. The isolation. And finally, the disbelief.

A million different emotions had beaten her down over

the last ninety unbearable days. By the time her race packet arrived, her only desire was to get out of Los Angeles. She was thankful she'd entered on a whim, when she saw the Half Marathon advertised. She usually only ran in the L.A. area but the San Francisco race sounded interesting and she'd always intended to enter, one day. At thirty-six, her involvement in running remained steadfast. In fact, through all the ups and downs in her life, athletic escapes were tantamount to sanity. And with the way she felt tonight, if by some rotten luck her car had broken down when she tried to leave L.A., she would have gladly run the distance.

She glanced at herself in the rearview mirror and marveled that what she'd been through was not detectable on her face. Her hazel eyes were a bit tired, but not drastically puffy. Her thick, sandy brown hair still shined as it rested on her shoulders. Though she felt beaten down, she was still holding her five-foot-eight frame together fairly well. She'd lost a few pounds, tilting toward the lean side of the scale, but she wasn't unhealthy.

She rolled down the window, letting in the cold manure smell of the cattle yards around Coalinga. Had she been drinking, the frigid stench spilling into her car would have sobered her. As it was, her overworked mind just ached more. And in the blackness of nowhere, as her tires hummed in cadence to the droning in her head, Beth knew, without a doubt, that where she was going couldn't possibly be worse than what she had left behind.

Beth pulled up to the curb at Fisherman's Wharf. It was just past seven in the morning and the sun, from somewhere above the clouds, was beginning to brighten the streets. The seagulls were already squawking at the fish vendors, who busied themselves for the day's trade, packing fish in icy beds, stoking fires under cauldrons of clam chowder, and cracking crab for tourists' cocktails. The vendors yelled back and forth to each other, comfortable in their habitat and fluid in their movements.

Scanning the merchant signs, Beth chose a diminutive diner touting "The West Coast's Best Seafood Omelets." She didn't order an omelet but instead chose coffee as black as her mood and toast just as dry.

There were three other patrons dining that early. A couple, probably married, bickered over travel arrangements at a booth. And a man with a beard long enough to rest in his lap sat at the counter, hunched over a newspaper.

Beth slid her keys into the pocket of her jeans and made a mental check of her vital signs as she sat down and ordered breakfast. Her heart ached just slightly more than her splitting head. Her eyes burned from crying between Coalinga and Los Banos. And her stomach threatened to refuse even the toast and coffee she'd just requested. The notion that she'd just driven five hundred miles was only now sinking in.

Now what? Her relationship had been over for over three months, but the nasty taste wasn't going away. The idea that she could leave her pain behind was obviously a foolish one. She knew she couldn't expect instant relief, but a change of scene was supposed to help people move on. It was worth a six-hour drive to find out. The Half Marathon was two weeks away, plenty of time to regroup. She would be concentrating on race preparation and training. She would have a lot on her mind, a new routine, and different surroundings to explore.

Beth was immediately jarred. In her haste to leave L.A., and her general lack of concentration, she hadn't made any plans for a hotel. Great. That was all she needed, no shower when she arrived and a hassle finding a place to stay. She'd thought that through pretty well.

She wrapped her hands around the mug of black sludge the waitress set in front of her and closed her eyes to the coffee, the diner, the city, and the whole fucking world. The piercing reality of her escape hurt more than she could bear and she wanted to block everything out. But in the shadow behind her eyes, she still existed. And that fact she couldn't escape.

"Are you all right?"

Beth looked up at the waitress. No, she wasn't all right. She was sitting in a diner five hundred miles from home and she wanted to jump off the Golden Gate Bridge but instead, she was just going to run a race and see if she could get thirteen more miles away from this ache.

"Coffee's too strong, isn't it? I'll make another pot," the waitress offered.

"No, that's okay. I need to go."

Beth paid the check and walked back to her car. She drove slowly west, toward Van Ness Street, watching the wharf start its daily commerce. Crafts merchants armed with jewelry, pottery, and T-shirts were setting up their stalls along the streets. The shops were opening and tourists were beginning to buy loaves of freshly baked sourdough bread and Golden Gate Bridge key chains.

The air felt different, crisper than L.A. The streets were up and down, not flat. Even the trees were dissimilar. And suddenly the murky charcoal cloud that hung behind Beth's eyes parted for a second, letting through a lone fragment of a thought. By removing herself from her home, she'd eliminated the constant triggers that jogged painful memories. She no longer occupied the rooms she'd shared with Stephanie. There were no familiar streets or houses. She would not pass cafés where they ate together or stores they shopped in. Certainly if she thought long enough the memories would come knifing their way back, but she was already beginning to have moments void of pain. And though fleeting, a nanosecond's reprieve was better than none.

She found Market Street and turned west. It had been a year since she'd been in San Francisco, but as cities went, it was an easy one to get around. If lost, a driver couldn't go too far without seeing water and recalibrating. And though it wasn't home, Castro Street felt strangely comfortable as she followed the cars streaming through the gay Mecca of Northern California. Anyone could be anyone, here. And right now, though Beth wasn't sure of most things, she knew at the very least that she was gay.

Chapter Two

Another cup of coffee felt as necessary as oxygen, so Beth found a parking space a few blocks east of Castro Street. The neighborhood was typical, rehabbed Victorian houses standing shoulder to shoulder with apartment buildings in the economy of space that was San Francisco. The façades were elaborate and the color schemes characteristic of the city. Many windows and porches displayed the rainbow flag, symbolizing gay unity.

It was Friday morning and most people were leaving for work. Beth walked down Liberty Street, relishing the warmth of the air in contrast to Fisherman's Wharf. People scurried to their cars, waved and kissed each other good-bye, walked dogs, and jogged past her. Beth unbuttoned her jacket, wishing she could take a run herself after hours jammed behind a steering wheel. Even in her haste to pack, she had remembered the most important items, her running clothes and shoes.

But the relief of a long, serenity-inducing run would have to wait. She needed to find a room, and even before that, she was headed for more java. A quick fix. She looked up at the layer of fog that hung over the city, and something close to a smile hovered at her lips. She was definitely not in Los Angeles. Gone was the knot in her stomach. The throb in her head was little more than a twinge. And she could breathe deeply for the first time in months.

Beth stepped inside a coffeehouse on Castro and ordered a double espresso. Her mouth had been ready for a cappuccino, but just as she started to give her order, a sharp spasm of anguish racked her chest and she hurried to choose the strongest potion available, hoping to quell the hurt.

As she sipped the earthy blend, she swore that vile word. "Stephanie."

Ten minutes later, her nerves steeled, she left the thick warmth of the coffeehouse and paused just outside the door. The sun was brighter than it had seemed when she hastened indoors, but the wind howled through her jacket and rattled a steel trash can next to her. A young man with a beautiful face, and fingers scratching his stubble, turned to smile at her. She smiled back, knowing his gesture was not a proposition of dalliance but an acknowledgment of their gay lifestyle. She felt comforted by that. For some, as small as it was, the Castro was a whole world, the encapsulation of all its inhabitants sought to make it: a safe haven, a lively bender, a political zone, a home. Right now, Beth thought she might want the Castro to be all those things.

She spent the next hour roaming up and down the streets. Ducking into clothing stores and jewelry shops, she explored and revisited. She wandered wherever a sign or a window display would take her. There was no calculated path, no mission. But somewhere in the deep recesses of her unconscious, masquerading as impulsiveness, she found herself charting a course though familiar ground. Without questioning the perception, she turned up a side street and walked the block and a half to a violet-and-yellow house. She stopped dead in front of the tall Victorian and gazed up toward the topmost dormer window.

Suddenly she was in that bedroom, with Stephanie, on one of their famous weekend getaways. A friend of Stephanie's was planning to be out of town and had offered the place to them, mailing a key. They'd driven up that day, spontaneous in their decision to flee normalcy. After a candlelit dinner on the Castro, they'd giggled all the way back to the house and stood kissing just inside the foyer.

Beth could still feel Stephanie's warmth coursing through her. She'd wanted her as she always did, stroking her spine and moving down around her backside to squeeze her cheeks.

"Mmm." Stephanie's whispers floated through time. "You always make me want you." She nibbled Beth's neck, pulling at her earlobe.

When they finally paused in their kisses, Beth led her upstairs. A shaft of moonlight painted the bedroom in gold, mingling with the flicker of a black-and-white movie they'd left playing on the television. Beth stopped Stephanie at the couch and kissed her again, gently pushing her down.

A pirate mutiny was being played out on the television. Distant, muted battle cries punctuated a dramatic score that raged on as Beth and Stephanie moved together on the couch. Beth was aroused beyond her sense of command, edging past the ability to control herself. With each moan from Stephanie, her chest felt as if it were swirling away.

Four or five commercial breaks later, the television treason still in its throes, Beth was under Stephanie. Though the windows were open and a damp breeze graced the room, they were wet with their own excitement. Beth laid her head back over the edge of the couch. Stephanie bent to her, running her tongue up her neck. Beth tilted up to meet her mouth and Stephanie reached a hand to the floor for support as she held Beth half off the couch. They finally slid onto the floor without ending their kiss, and Stephanie made love to her in an unhurried, slow rhythm.

As Beth broke through the first waves of arousal, she whispered, "God, I want you."

She had her arms over her head and was clutching the corner of the woven rug underneath her. Stephanie was between her legs, arms wrapped around Beth's thighs. Her mouth drove Beth insane. She could feel those lips trailing kisses along her inner thighs as she swelled and got unbearably wetter. She lifted her hips and felt the weight of Stephanie's upper body. The sensation was powerful. She inhaled deeply and pulled at the rug, trying to relax. Part of her was racing toward orgasm, the rest trying to savor what Stephanie was doing. That constant push/pull drove her crazy every time they made love. She always wanted to come as soon as she felt Stephanie's breath between her legs, all the while trying to slow down and enjoy.

Whether it had been hours or minutes, Beth wasn't sure, staring up at that room now, years later. Deep down, in the back of her mind, she was still reeling from the shocking joy of that encounter, dragged back to the place only Stephanie could take her. She could remember almost nothing else about that weekend, or others like it. All she could focus on was the memory of their bodies, the feeling of Stephanie's hair as her cheeks brushed the insides of her thighs. Beth remembered gazing down at her and placing her hands around the back of Stephanie's head. Arching against her, she fell deep into a rapture she could barely hang on to.

It was incredible. The waves inside her grew until she could not longer resist or delay and was overcome with contractions. She moaned with each spasm, groping for something to hang on to. Stephanie matched her bucking, holding on to her frenzy until her gasping slowed, then she moved up the length of Beth's body and buried her face in her neck.

"My God," Beth whispered, breathing in slow heaves, marveling at the sensation she'd just been given. She closed her eyes and kissed Stephanie's shoulder. "What are you doing to me?"

"Hopefully making you feel good."

"Good is not the word."

They'd lain there for a while, holding each other.

Beth stroked the hair at Stephanie's temple and looked into her eyes. "I love you so much. I don't want to go home. I want to stay here until we grow old."

"I think that's a perfect idea," Stephanie said. "Then no one could bother us."

"We say this every time we go out of town, don't we?" Beth whispered.

Stephanie smiled. "Yes, we do. But there's nothing wrong with that. I want you all to myself."

All to myself. All to myself. Those last words rang in Beth's ears as she blinked at the dormer window. Filled with misery, she whispered, "If you had only meant it, Stephanie."

How quickly passion and love had turned into pain and deceit. She stumbled away from the memory of that night, turning up another street and walking blindly past cars and houses and people who seemed to have wonderful lives. As she roamed around the Castro, she questioned whether coming to San Francisco had been such a great idea. The day suddenly felt colder, or perhaps the chill was internal. Stopping at the intersection of Hancock and Noe, she craned upward to contemplate the fog bank moving stalwartly toward the east. Wouldn't it be nice to hop a ride and float on that hazy gray quilt to some far-off land whose laws forbade pain and suffering, lying and cheating, deceit and manipulation? Well, at least to a place where there were no painful memories stored, and where everyone left her alone.

Or maybe she'd just drive over to Sausalito.

Beth laughed out loud, marveling at the madness that coursed nonstop through her tortured mind of late. She hugged her sweater closer to her body and continued walking. Maybe a little insanity was what she needed. It would numb like an anesthetic, tempering pain and confusion, and allowing her a sense of calmness and serenity, however false.

As she sauntered through the neighborhood, her spirits began to lift. The houses she passed were colorfully resplendent, each a neat and tidy expression of someone's personality. It was obvious that their owners took great pride in how they were decorated and kept up, and not simply because real estate in this part of San Francisco was very valuable.

Beth had always liked this city; it had such character and ambience. Her parents had brought her here many times. She remembered playing in Golden Gate Park, running the length of Fisherman's Wharf, and walking the streets of Chinatown. And when she was old enough to drive, she'd made many trips, mostly with friends, sometimes with lovers. Every trip felt familiar and comfortable as she rediscovered her favorite neighborhoods again and again, witnessing their changes over the years. Even the pangs she'd just felt remembering Stephanie and the violet-and-yellow Victorian didn't quell her love of the city.

A slight smile broke across her lips as she thought about that. In San Francisco, she could feel at home yet leave behind so much she didn't want to drag around anymore. If she wanted a new beginning, she couldn't think of a better place to make a start. She could see herself living here, even being happy here. One day. Sometime. She had to believe she wouldn't always feel this way. Sorrows passed. People survived. Wounds healed.

She paused to get her bearings, staring up at a huge, old house on the corner. It sat stoically, painted white with light blue trim. It looked to have many rooms, with rainbow flags flapping from half of them. A sign caught her eye. In big, bold letters it read ROOM FOR RENT. BY WEEK OR MONTH. OWN BATHROOM. SEE ALDER BECKMAN.

Spontaneity, Beth knew, was sometimes born from the need to eliminate pain, driving people to do something, anything, as long as it offered change. She had intended, all along, to return to Fisherman's Wharf to find a hotel, but instead she walked up the steps of the old house and rang the doorbell. As she waited for an answer, she accepted that she was acting on instinct and that very few of her recent actions were dictated by sensible planning or conscious decisions. But what she did realize was that she was smack-dab in the middle of some sort of subconscious trek.

Leaving Los Angeles without proper packing or planning, ending up in San Francisco well before the race she'd entered, on this doorstep at this moment in time, didn't make much sense. And the fact that she had no idea what to expect and, moreover, that it didn't matter, was unusual, to say the least. Beth was okay with the unpredictable, up to a point, but she'd never handed her fate over to chance this way.

As the doorknob creaked counterclockwise, she gave herself the option to turn around and march back the way she came. But her feet stayed where they were and she decided that whatever adventure lay ahead was better than anything back home.

A woman of about fifty smiled from the threshold. She was tall and thin with wisps of gray hair flowing through a long, auburn mane. "Yes?"

"I was wondering about the sign you have up there in the window." Beth smiled.

"Well, there's one room. It's small, but it has its own bathroom."

Beth absorbed the relevant details. $500 per week or $1800 by the month. Renovated. Clean. She was almost ready to say no before the woman waved a welcoming arm.

"Come on in off the stoop."

Beth followed her into a beautifully decorated living room. Thick Berber carpet covered the large expanse of room. A tapestry couch sat against the front wall. Beyond this, a large picture window offered a view of the front street. An antique mahogany piano dominated the side wall and an arched opening led to a dining room. The dining room opened into an ivy-filled solarium.

"Sit." The woman gestured toward the couch. "I'm Alder Beckman. I own the place."

Beth shook her hand. "I'm Beth. You have a beautiful house."

"Thank you. It's been a lot of work. Where are you from?"

"Los Angeles."

"How is the City of Angels?"

"It's five hundred miles away."

Adler scanned Beth's face, then cracked a smile. "Yes, it is. Well, are you looking for a long-term or short-term situation?"

"Short term. I just needed to get away from L.A. I'm running the Half Marathon in two weeks."

"It's a popular race. You'll enjoy it."

"I hadn't really intended to come up this early, but the idea of staying a little while sounds pretty good."

Beth didn't know why she felt she could open up to

this woman. She'd just met her. The fact that she was a total stranger did make it easier. Alder had a wiser-than-her-years look in her eyes. Beth liked that.

"Well, there are nine of us in the other five bedrooms," Alder said. "The people who live here are longtimers. It's a pretty good group. They like the break on their rent when that small room is rented."

"May I see the room?"

Alder jumped to her feet. "Sure. This way."

Beth followed her up an immense staircase, extra wide and so solid in its construction that there was not one creak. There were two bedrooms at the first landing.

"Everyone's at work right now," Alder said. "But this is Keith's room and that's Gina and Diane's room." She led Beth up the next flight. "The rest of us are up here."

She pointed out the bedrooms on the third floor landing and named the renters. Beth immediately gave up trying to remember who was where. She would have an easier time remembering names once she could see their faces.

Alder paused near the end of the hall. "My room's here."

Beth glanced around. "And the room for rent?"

Alder gestured into her own room. "Right here with me, in my room, sweetie."

Beth blinked, which caused Alder to laugh a deep belly laugh. It was the kind of laugh that immediately warmed others. It came from deep inside a happy, contented soul.

"I'm joking." Alder recovered. "Anyway, it's much funnier when I use that line on the straight women that come around. Come on, follow me."

At the far end of the hallway, Alder opened a door that Beth had originally thought was a closet. But when Alder pulled on a dangling light chain, she could see a narrow staircase that led upward to a smaller, fourth floor. The musty smell of timeworn mahogany filled her nostrils as she ascended to the top of the staircase, where a small attic room with an even smaller bathroom awaited, patient and unassuming. It felt demure but tranquil.

"The room's tiny, but it's private." Alder walked to the only window, which faced the street. "You can just catch a glimpse of…well, mostly rooftops and fog. But there's fresh air, nevertheless."

A pine-framed queen bed dominated the room, its headboard at the window. On it lay a teal and purple patchwork quilt. There was a dresser against the left wall, a small closet on the right, and a rocking chair in one corner. The middle of the oak-slatted floor was covered with a rug that was well past its prime but still thick enough to counter drafts.

"It's very cute," Beth said. "I'd like to stay for a week." She would move to a hotel closer to the race the second week.

Alder smiled. "Great. Cash is better than a check."

"Cash is fine. Do you need an ID from me or anything?"

"I'll get it later. I like to have everyone's names and addresses, but as far as security goes," Alder paused for drama, "I don't think you're the bad type."

"You're a trusting soul."

Alder held up a finger. "I'm a good reader of character." With that, she traded a front door key for Beth's money and said, "If you want to go get your stuff, I'll make coffee. Or do you prefer tea?"

Beth smiled. "Coffee, thank you."

After she'd parked her car closer, she retrieved her hastily packed duffel bag. By the time she got back upstairs to the room, Alder had placed fresh towels on the bed. As Beth began unpacking, she heard footsteps on the stairs and Alder entered with two mugs in hand.

"Takes the chill off, opens the eyeballs." She handed Beth

a mug and sipped from the other. "I wanted to let you know a few things. There's no maid service, so the sheets and towels are your responsibility. The washer is downstairs on the back porch, through the kitchen. Everyone buys his or her own detergent. And the regular stuff applies. Eat what you buy. Throw away or recycle what you're done with. Oh, and yes, I don't know if this is good luck or bad timing for you, but the Coop's having a party tomorrow night. Of course, you're very welcome, but don't feel obligated to attend."

Puzzled, Beth asked, "The Coop?"

Alder chuckled. "That's what everyone calls this place. Anyway, every few months we throw a party, and if you're feeling up to it, it's usually quite fun…if not totally amusing." She started for the door. "Well, I'll get out of your hair now. Seems like you might want some privacy."

Beth was about to disagree, mostly because she was raised by polite parents who taught their children to be just as polite, but Alder was already departing down the stairs.

Beth spent most of the rest of the day lying on the bed. Face up, she stared at the ceiling and let her thoughts roam. She found herself strangely soothed by the noises of the house, creaks in the walls, muffled talk, a faraway washer and dryer. People entered the front door. There was laughter and the sound of clunking up and down the stairs.

She must have fallen asleep for a few hours because when she woke up, the light in her room had faded and she could hear increased activity throughout the house. To her surprise she was hungry. Recently, she'd lost her appetite and sometimes skipped meals for days in a row. Tonight, however, she was tempted by the thought of food.

Beth pulled on a clean pair of jeans and went downstairs, trying to decide what she felt like, a snack or a serious meal. On her way out, she stopped by the living room and met a few of the Coop residents, two women, both around thirty years old, and a man more firmly rooted in his twenties. They were on the floor, putting together final touches on an elaborate sign.

One of the woman looked up from her handiwork. "You're Beth?" At Beth's nod, she said, "I'm Judy and this is my wife, Fran."

Beth recalled that they shared the room across from Alder.

"This is Keith."

The young man flashed a bright white, toothy grin.

Beth gestured toward the sign, genuinely curious. "What are you working on?"

"Keith was commissioned to come up with an AIDS awareness poster. We're just helping with the last details. It's due tomorrow."

Keith resumed cutting some scrap paper. "Judy, I didn't know you were my spokesperson. You yap more than any of the queens I know."

Judy teased back, "That's not possible. If it weren't for your scuttlebutt network, no one would have any gossip."

Fran shook her head. "I can see I'm going to have to separate you two again if we ever want to get this done. So Beth, what do you think of the poster?"

Keith held it up. Four condoms stood erect, side by side. Each was a different neon color. Blue, red, yellow, and green. The wording read I COME IN COLORS, DO YOU?

"Think it's too subtle?" he asked.

Beth laughed. "It's a great idea. You sure got the message across."

"Are you off to dinner?" Fran asked.

"Could you hear my stomach growling?"

Judy chimed in. "I thought that was just Keith's brain coming up with another idea."

Keith raised a scissored hand and dismissed everyone with a wave. "Thank you, thank you. Yes, they do come rather frequently."

"Any café suggestions?" Beth queried.

It was Judy who volunteered, "There's a great Mexican restaurant three blocks down Seacliff Avenue. And there's a coffee shop on Brand, one block before Castro."

Beth opened the front door as she thanked them, saying she'd try the coffee shop.

Fran called, "Welcome to the Coop!"

CHAPTER THREE

Saturday morning, Beth lay in bed willing the time to pass after another loathsome night of fitful sleep. Her body was racked with exhaustion, brought on by so many sleepless nights that she'd lost count, but she was unable to shut off her mind. Images kept stabbing at her brain. Bodies tangled in sweaty sex, groping and clutching in the sounds of lust. Groans building to orgasm amid the thrashing of rumpled sheets. And what made a normally alluring jumble of mental pictures so wretched was that one of the bodies belonged to the woman she used to share a bed with, but the other was not her own.

Beth tormented herself with relentless visions of unfaithfulness for hours every night, a nocturnal purgatory made worse by cascades of tears that left her with a throbbing headache. The pounding in her temples this morning was nothing unusual. She tried to relax, listening to the morning sounds of a strange house in a strange neighborhood. But she gave up at six thirty and got out of bed. Hoping a brisk run around the Castro would exorcise the demons from her mind, she pulled on her running gear and crept out of the house.

The chill of the air gripped her lungs during the first mile, but as she began warming up, the only symptoms of the cold San Francisco morning were her numb ears. The hills slowed her on the way up and then pounded her knees on the way down, but overall, she felt pretty good. Her calves had tightened from the climbing so she walked another mile or so to stretch them out before returned to the Coop. Judging by her watch, she figured she'd run about five miles.

The residents were just beginning to stir when she climbed the stairs to her room. The hot shower she eased herself into felt marvelous. Though she would gladly have remained under the pleasant massaging stream of hot water, she grudgingly stepped out into her Lilliputian bathroom. Its black-and-white tile floor felt cool on her feet. The temptation to crawl back into bed was a strong one, but she was fairly sure the nightmares of Stephanie would revisit.

Since that particular mental button was not one she could turn off easily, she threw on denim shorts and Bass sandals and a thin, faded T-shirt. Normally, despite firm breasts, she wore a bra, but forgoing the support today made sense for two reasons: she didn't care and, well, she didn't care. She stuffed her just-past-shoulder-length hair into a baseball cap and padded down the stairs.

She'd heard rumblings as she returned from her run, but no one had actually come out of their rooms. She glanced around to see if anyone was in the kitchen or dining area, just in case she could make a friendly offer of coffee. But she was the first to rise. She wasn't surprised. It was Saturday and most of the residents had been up the previous night until past one in the morning. No one had been loud, but the house had carried sounds of a television, chatter from the living room, the front door opening and closing countless times, and the same, soothing clunking up and down the stairs.

She left the house quietly and hiked back toward the Castro, stopping at the first café she found. Two cups of leaded and a newspaper helped kill an hour, and a brisk, aimless walk around the shopping district dispatched another. Upon her return at ten thirty, the house had arisen. Beth met up with Judy and Fran in the kitchen and fielded an offer of more coffee. They'd made a house-sized pot.

"What the hell," Beth said. "I've already had two cups, but three's a charm. I'd love some."

Judy patted Beth's shoulder. She had workout clothes on, tight shorts and a tank top. Fran was still in her robe. Alder sat at the kitchen table with two other women and two men. She introduced Beth to everyone.

Gina was plump and busty, around thirty years old, with long, thick locks of dark brown hair that spiraled down her back. Her lover, Diane, was a little older, tall and thin, with a blond bob haircut. She looked to be ready for a quick game of tennis. Black-haired Dan was in his late twenties and quietly engrossed in a newspaper. Keith waved a hand while wiping his mouth clean of jelly from a bite of toast.

After the small talk died down, Beth excused herself to the back porch. She'd spied the quiet spot as soon as she came into the kitchen. It was deserted, which was perfect for her, but situated just off the kitchen, close enough to make her feel she wasn't being too unsociable. The porch steps led down to a modest backyard full of flowers. Two parallel paths led toward the back fence. On either side of the paths, flowers of every color bloomed unabashedly. Beth noticed right away that the arrangement of colors was in prism order, the colors of the rainbow. The whole backyard was warm, bright, and full of gay unity.

Up on the porch, four patio chairs were huddled around an old wooden table that told its own story. A sense of well-being came over her as she sat down and took in the imprints left by good times and friendship. Clumps of dried wax spoke of candlelit nights gone by. Circular stains marked the ghosts of bottles of wine and beer. And someone had carved the initials L.F. + L.S. in the bleached, timeworn slats. The columns that held up the porch's roof showed signs of the same past parties. Small pieces of discolored streamers were still impaled on rusted thumbtacks. Strands of tiny Christmas tree lights dangled across the ceiling, moist with the morning's dew, while old, ratty speakers, mounted to the corners of the ceiling, sat mute but hopeful.

Beth smiled. It was nice to sit here among the memories the porch quietly held. She loved the fact that everything she looked at was new to her, unburdened by association. She could feel the muscles in her neck relaxing, and with the release of tension, her headache started to fade. A cackle of laughter from the kitchen broke in on her reflections and she tuned in to the idle banter of her new roommates. The animated gossip meant little to her, since she knew none of the players. The chatter washed through her brain, pushing out thoughts of home. And that was good.

When a new voice loudly disrupted the flow of conversation, Beth turned as a strikingly beautiful woman somewhere in her thirties careened into the kitchen and crashed into Alder's chair. With a playful whoop, she grabbed the older woman in a bear hug, saying, "Come here, I wanna hug your neck."

As each member of the household greeted the new arrival, Beth stayed where she was, watching through the window. She found herself riveted to the sight. The woman was at least six feet tall, four inches taller than Beth, with shoulder-length blond hair. Her beyond-white teeth flashed a luxurious smile. She had an incredible body, broad shoulders, a flat stomach, and long, long legs. And standing out even more than her looks was the shamelessly brazen way she entertained everyone. She gracefully greeted one person after the next, hugging, joking, and being quite dazzling. The kitchen seemed to light up and all the sluggish Saturday morning motions picked up energy in her presence.

Beth was captivated, hardly aware that she was staring as the woman moved around the room, happily engaged in what could only be described as working the crowd. It seemed as if she was purposely bestowing her quintessence upon everyone. And what fascinated Beth was that although the display appeared deliberate, it couldn't have seemed more natural. Her air of celebrity appeared to be an extension of her confident personality, something she carried around with her every waking moment. Beth imagined she probably mastered it in her sleep, as well.

She began to grow uncomfortable. Like a classroom student at the mercy of an inquisitive instructor, she tried to look invisible so the woman did not notice her and come parading out to the porch. She looked down at the weathered wooden tabletop, pondering the events going on inside. There was something about dramatically gregarious people that she just couldn't relate to. Well, she actually could relate, she just couldn't emulate. Who couldn't appreciate the type of person who commanded a room full of people through sheer effervescence?

To the more conservative Beth, such behavior was definitely over the top. Too much. Though it was obvious that everyone being entertained in the Coop's kitchen knew this woman, she still had them captivated. The more Beth felt mesmerized by her, the more she detested feeling that way. She just couldn't figure out why she was so riveted. The woman was not quite brash and definitely not rude. Pert was too mild. Then Beth settled on a description: vainly cavalier.

Yes, that summed her up perfectly. If Beth had to guess,

she would say this woman had never spent a single minute of her life wondering about her own faults and flaws. She knew she was wonderful and expected others to recognize this too. Suddenly the back door opened and Beth inwardly winced. Discovered.

"Well, here's the new addition to the Coop."

The fact that was a declaration and not a question or polite greeting irritated Beth. She smiled vaguely, determined to appear unimpressed. The tall woman flung herself down in one of the wooden chairs, kicking her feet up onto the tabletop. As they landed, her heel dislodged a piece of old candle wax, causing it to fly off the porch.

"My name's Mary," she said.

"Beth." She was relieved to see Alder had followed Mary out onto the porch.

"Don't scare off our newest roommate, Mary." Alder was motherly in her tone.

"I wouldn't dream of it." Mary flashed that luxurious smile again and Beth noticed that her eyes were a light olive green. Mary went on, "Is this a long-term or short-term rooming thing?"

Alder began to answer but Beth beat her to it. "Short-term," she said a little tersely. What nerve. She was annoyed at this woman's pompousness and irked at her own prim reaction.

If Mary noticed any malevolence directed toward her, she ignored it. "Not so short-term that you won't be able to make the Coop's party tonight, I trust."

Alder sighed. "Beth will come if she wants to, but it might not be her cup of tea."

"I can't think of a person who wouldn't like your party, Alder. It's got something for everyone. Drinks for the drinkers, soda for the steppers, quiet nooks and crannies for the chatty ones, and loud music for dancers." Mary wagged a finger, declaring, "Why, I think I even saw half the members of the Castro Chess Club at your last bash."

Alder chuckled quietly and turned to Beth. "Your room will be quite removed from the noise if you choose not to attend. Only the first two floors are party accessible. The top two are off-limits."

Beth nodded, imagining how much better it would be if she were up there right now, avoiding this conversation. She didn't want to offend her kind landlady, but she wasn't in the mood to socialize. Besides, she had nothing to celebrate at a party, unless a failed relationship counted.

"Who wouldn't want to come?" Mary looked into Beth's eyes. "Jay plays the best music in the Castro."

Alder elaborated. "Jay spins records at some of the bars here. He's very popular. As long as I ask him to play music, I don't have to worry about getting a full house. He comes with his own crowd."

"Jay wouldn't miss your shindigs for anything, Alder. Nor would anyone else. It's a legacy I'm afraid you're stuck with."

Beth was relieved that the focus of the conversation had drifted away from her. Listening to the banter between Alder and Mary, she did admit that although the thought of attending the party was abhorrent, it could be exactly what she needed most. Social medicine for a misanthropic shut-in. Somewhere inside her lay a party girl-in-waiting. It hadn't been that many years ago that she had thrown a shindig or three. But that part of her world had been severed when the rest of her life took a different turn. Maybe she needed to try and get back to some of the things she used to enjoy.

The party sounded interesting, at the very least, and it would be a great pain diverter, but she didn't know anyone and didn't feel very talkative. Then again, she didn't paint herself out to be a wallflower. She was quite popular in her circles back home, making friends fairly easily. The last time she was single, she'd dated interesting woman. No one seemed to find her boring, but at the moment she was so unsociable she felt horribly close to dullard status. Especially with partygoers like Mary-in-your-face. She really wasn't up to dealing with the likes of someone that ribald.

A party was the last thing Beth had on her mind when she'd gotten in her Mercedes the day before. Other than training for the race, she could think of nothing else she cared to do. A party would have been bottom of her list, which, if she wrote one, would look like this:

1. Brood in some dark place, alone, for hours.
2. Mope about in sweats and a dirty T-shirt, alone, for hours.
3. Anguish over the pain of being stabbed in the heart, alone, for hours.

Going to a party would call for things she wasn't really prepared to do, like showering, dressing, and socializing. She took inventory. The shower she could handle, but she hadn't exactly thought to bring "nice" clothes. She looked down at what she was wearing. The thin, faded T-shirt and denim shorts couldn't be making an acceptable impression, let alone the threadbare baseball cap and the absence of her bra. In the cool morning air, she was now very conscious of the latter and, if Mary's candid stares were any indication, she wasn't the only one.

Beth's thoughts became abruptly fragmented as she registered her name being spoken. She blinked. "Pardon me?"

Mary said, "It's one of the few chances you'll get to see the Teddy contest."

"At every party Jay picks a Teddy Pendergrass song to lip-synch to," Alder explained. "The most shameless guests partake."

"The most fun-loving ones," Mary corrected.

"Much to the amusement of everyone else." Alder got up and smacked Mary on the back. "Enough about the party. And enough with bugging Beth. Leave her to her quiet Saturday morning."

Mary obligingly got up and followed Alder toward the door but not before looking back at Beth once again. Their eyes locked for a moment. Beth inwardly prepared for another verbal joust in which she was loath to participate. But instead of making a cocky remark, Mary curved her lips in a sincere smile.

"It was nice to meet you, Beth."

For the first time since she'd careened into the Coop, her show ended and her words were suddenly quite unpretentious. And just as that appealing fact occurred to Beth, Mary slipped inside the house.

Beth sat there, confused. She'd spent the last few minutes as some kind of verbal quarry for Mary. The woman had sucked her into a performance that made all that banter seem routine, when it was entirely of Mary's composition. Beth hadn't solicited inclusion, she had rather repelled it. But Mary had cornered her effortlessly, just as she did everyone else, making them all play their roles in her script. Beth resented that, and she was equally irritated that just when she'd had enough of Mary's mischief, she was thrown by the sincerity of that last statement.

Trouble. That woman was trouble.

❖

"Mary's quite a character." Alder sat down on the end of Beth's bed after being waved in from the doorway. "I hope she wasn't too much for you to take your first morning here."

Beth laughed. "No."

"She's kind of like a butterfly. Well, an insane butterfly. But she's really a good soul. It's just hard to contain her and no one has ever been able to change her." Alder reflected over what Beth imagined were innumerous escapades. "I can't imagine anyone wanting to. But if she bothers you, let me know."

"I'm a big girl," Beth said, feeling like the opposite. She'd spent the rest of the morning lying on her bed so tired and depressed that she had no desire to do anything, even if she could think of something to do. Mary was the least of her problems. "Don't worry, I can handle her."

"I'm sure you can."

"Do you mind if I stay here a little longer than a week?" Beth wasn't sure why she suddenly wanted to change her plans. Maybe it was something about the family feel of the Coop. She felt safe here.

"Of course not." Alder paused a moment, and then asked, "Did you come to San Francisco or leave Los Angeles?"

It was cryptic but Beth knew what she meant. "I left Los Angeles." Which was the truth, but a horrible nagging started inside.

She knew she had to fight that sick need to get back home, just in case Stephanie hadn't meant what she said. She'd spent the past three months clinging to that possibility, and now understood she was simply in denial. Stephanie wasn't coming back to her. That was the reality.

"You're not the first," Alder said, leaving an opening if Beth wanted to take it.

And maybe she did. It was time to face facts, and a little confession might help. "I needed to get away from a woman."

"Sometimes being away does wonders. And I'm not just saying that to keep you here."

"I had to get away. Anywhere. I mean, here's not just anywhere. It's nice here."

"That's as good a reason as any to stay." Alder studied Beth for a moment. Slowly she said, "If this is your chosen sanctuary, then be empowered by it. And don't call her, because you will say things and hear things that will set you back."

Beth nodded mutely, wondering if Alder could read minds. She did want to call Stephanie sometimes. Out of habit, and in her weaker moments.

Alder added, "Maybe you had to drive this far away to get yourself back." She patted Beth on the knee and got up. "I hope we see you later."

Beth smiled. "I hope so, too."

That evening the household gathered to put up decorations, clean the kitchen, set out recycling containers, and ready chests that would later hold ice. Music rolled from the stereo and most were singing along.

Beth spent a couple hours helping with the preparations and then went out to buy more beer, soda, and ice. Alder had declined her offer to buy the supplies, but Beth pointed out that she hadn't paid for the coffee she'd been drinking since she arrived, nor for the dinner Alder had supplied while they decorated. Diane, who was in fact the tennis player she looked like, and Gina, who was studying to be a therapist, went along for the beer run. By seven thirty, the drinks were on ice, the house was ready, and Jay had arrived to set up his equipment.

As Beth went back upstairs to shower and change, she realized she felt better than she'd thought she would. Since Alder had left her room earlier that morning, Beth had been thinking about what she'd said. *If this is your chosen sanctuary, then be empowered by it. And don't call her, because you will say things and hear things that will set you back.*

Either Alder was very wise, or Beth reeked of her own plight. Whichever it was, she'd decided that assisting in the house decorating was a busy-chore that would pass some time. What she'd found were very congenial housemates who made her feel remarkably at home. Amazingly, Beth was actually looking forward to the party. Startled by her change of heart, she stepped from the shower, shampoo-scented steam swirling around her. She wrapped the towel snug and swiped at the foggy mirror over the sink. Upon examination, her eyes screamed for some Visine, but otherwise, she looked passable.

And there was something else. She studied her reflection, trying to identify what had changed. The numb look, she decided. She'd grown so accustomed to the frozen tension in her mouth and brow, she'd forgotten how she looked when she relaxed. She smiled experimentally. The thaw was far from complete. She wasn't sure if she would ever feel completely whole again, but the calm warmth of her expression made her believe for the first time that all was not lost.

Chapter Four

B eth. You look wonderful." Dan, dressed in blue shorts and white tank top with a lei around his neck, was slopping guacamole into a ceramic bowl.

Beth self-consciously inspected her clothes. The choice had been easy. Her black Levi's and tight, plain white T-shirt were the only things she'd packed that weren't either too grungy or too wrinkled. Her breasts weren't large, a solid B-cup, but she was a little self-conscious of the way they announced themselves in the tautness of the shirt. She'd dropped close to ten pounds because of Stephanie, the loss trimming up her figure, but even so, the shirt was noticeably snug. She thought of running back upstairs to change, but felt a hand on her shoulder.

"Grab a drink, Beth." Alder smiled warmly. She wore a spruce green turtleneck and khaki pants. "Go out to the coolers and help yourself. Hell, you bought the stuff, why am I telling you?"

Beth smiled. "Would you like anything?"

"A light beer would be divine, thanks."

Beth squeezed past the people milling about the back door, excusing herself as she made her way toward the coolers at the far end of the porch. She could hear laughter down in the backyard. The darkness was punctuated only by a smattering of candles and hanging Christmas lights, but as her eyes adjusted she made out a large group of moonlit people by some roses. The Coop party had drawn quite a crowd. At least forty people stood watching Jay, the DJ, when she returned to the front living room with the beers she'd fished out of the cooler.

"All you queens and homogirlies are gonna love the music I put together tonight." Jay kept up a steady chatter as he made his music choices. "You're gonna think you're in your fave local bar, but the only difference is, you don't have to tip for the booze."

When he cranked the first song of the night, many began dancing immediately, while others bobbed their heads to the beat.

Alder took the beer Beth offered. "I'm glad you decided to join us. And I'm glad you extended your stay. There are lots of fun things to do here and nice places to go."

"The nicest thing about this city is that it feels completely different from Los Angeles," Beth stated simply.

"That it does. I lived in L.A. for many years, but I always thought I needed to be up here. I had a meager job back there, a circle of friends that were probably not that great for me, and generally my life wasn't what I needed it to be. Anyway, one day I just left. I sold off most of my belongings and figured I could do better here."

"It takes guts to leave."

"I guess you'd know."

"Me? I just left on a…vacation of sorts," Beth said. "You packed up your life and went."

"There's really no difference." Alder looked reflective. "You needed to get away just like I did. The first step is realizing a change has to happen."

"Like starting over after a breakup."

When Beth didn't elaborate any further, Alder changed direction. "What part of L.A. do you call home?"

"Well, that's a good question. Right now I'm not sure." Beth stared at the beer label. "I pay the mortgage in Long Beach."

"Is your ex still living in the house?"

"No, she moved across town a few months ago."

"How long were you together?"

"A little more than three years."

Alder clinked her bottle against Beth's. "Hey, no more L.A. talk."

"Agreed." Beth leaned toward her. "Say, why is this place called the Coop?"

"Oh, it's just a joke. It comes from 'chicken coop.'"

"Why on Earth would it be called that?"

"Well, I'm almost too embarrassed to say. No one remembers the originator, but it was nicknamed the Coop because it's said that if you stay here long enough, you eventually get laid."

Beth knew her eyes were wide. She and Alder both started laughing at once. They watched the crowd through the next few songs. Beth appreciated the fact that Alder didn't pressure her for more information. She seemed to sense when to back off.

Impulsively, Beth voiced the thought that plagued her. "Do you think it could be called running away?"

Alder volunteered an experienced smile, the kind that made it clear that she'd faced this question before. "It's only considered running away if you avoid dealing with whatever you had to get away from."

The music ended and Jay yelled into his mic, asking the crowd if they wanted more music. They responded with suggestions and cheers.

"Anytime you want to talk about it…" Alder offered.

Beth managed a smile. "It's like a bad movie. And I only talk about bad movies over coffee."

"Well," Alder said, holding up her beer bottle, "this certainly isn't coffee."

Beth checked her watch. It was close to ten. "People sure don't waste time getting to your party."

"When there's free food, no one feels the need to make an entrance. Plus, it's pretty much the same crowd every party. Everyone looks forward to seeing each other."

"Kinda like church without the guilt."

Alder laughed her booming laugh. "We come from similar backgrounds. Listen, enjoy yourself to the hilt and don't regret a moment of it." She raised her bottle. "To an absolutely great, to-the-hilt evening."

Beth's glass met hers with a clink. "Regrets be damned."

Some time later, she wandered into the dining room and quickly found herself embroiled in a discussion with two women rugby players. Vicki was tall and wiry, and Candy was the more muscular of the pair. They were trying to recruit her. Even though the conversation wasn't deeply engrossing, she was enjoying herself. Between Alder and the rugby women, she'd met quite a few people throughout the house, all friendly and inquisitive. Her mood was higher than she could have imagined. She checked her watch. It was past eleven thirty and she was still enjoying herself.

"You could just come out and see if you like it," Vicki said.

"I'm sure it's a great sport," Beth conceded. "It's just that I have something against compressed vertebrae."

Candy shrugged. "That doesn't happen…that often."

"We play every Sunday. At Perkins Park." Vicki continued

trying to convince her. "You'd be a perfect candidate. You're probably fast, and we need fast women."

"Don't we all." Candy chuckled.

"Hear, hear," Vicky said and they raised their bottles to toast.

Before Beth could take a sip, she felt someone squeeze her elbow and turned to see Mary flash a spectacular Cheshire Cat grin.

"You came." She looked genuinely happy.

Jarred, Beth hesitated a moment, and her defenses immediately went up. She didn't want to be put on the spot again, compelled to fit in with Mary's agenda, whatever it was.

"I did," she replied. Her tone couldn't have been flatter, but Mary didn't seem to notice.

She and the rugby women knew each other and immediately started comparing notes about a game. "We're trying to recruit this one, here," Vicki said, tapping Beth on the shoulder.

Mary shook her head. "I'd like to have a few moments with her before she gets her first nosebleed."

Candy chortled. "Don't scare her off. Rugby's not that violent."

"Compared to the unrest in the Middle East, I guess you're right." Mary pulled Beth's elbow. "I'm gonna steal her for a minute, okay?"

"What makes you think I want to follow you?" Beth murmured as she was drawn away.

"Consider it a public service." Mary stopped long enough to smile. "Come on, they're rugby players, for goodness sakes. They're all maniacs, with hospital records to prove it. Plus, I wanted to talk to you."

They passed the kitchen, where a mob was crushed up

against the kitchen appliances. The living room was just as packed as the kitchen, but the music was blaring much louder.

"Even sardines would get claustrophobic." Mary turned toward the base of the staircase, by the front door. "Let's sit here."

She plopped down on the second step, leaning against the railing. Beth sat on the third step wondering what Mary wanted.

"I'm really glad you decided to come," Mary said.

A polite response was called for, but Beth wasn't sure that this brash woman deserved one. "Why?"

Mary tilted her head back slightly as if thinking, *Aha.* "Because I didn't get a chance to sit and talk with you this morning."

"You seemed to do quite a bit of talking," Beth retorted.

Mary appeared unfazed. "And you didn't."

Beth sorted through possible responses, the most immediate ones being, *I don't like to be a party to such an overbearing diatribe* or *You were talking so much, I'm surprised you even noticed I wasn't.* But before she could pick an answer, Mary offered her own take.

"Strangers tell me I come on too strong sometimes. Hell, who am I kidding? My friends say that, too."

"I'm sure you only find amusement in that, not humility." Beth heard herself and realized she'd been a little too sharp. She felt guilty for throwing such a barb, but keeping her dukes up still seemed prudent.

"You're a hard nut to crack, Miss Beth."

"Tough shell, I guess."

"I guess."

"So," Beth wanted to change the subject, "what would we have talked about?"

"You mean this morning?"

"Yes, if we'd sat down and had a real conversation."

Mary smiled. "Like, where are you from?"

"Los Angeles."

"How long are you here?"

"A couple of weeks."

Mary paused. "Why are you here?"

Beth sat silent, thinking, then slowly replied, "I need to be away."

Mary raised her eyebrow. "From?"

"Los Angeles."

"Well, I don't know much about you, but I do know that you're adept at circular conversations." Mary flashed her beyond-white teeth.

She was obviously joking, but this time Beth didn't feel that it was malicious. She shrugged. "I guess we're back to square one."

"It's a woman," Mary said. "You need time away from someone, so you came up here."

"God, is it that obvious?" Beth thought to say it out loud, then realized with shock that she *had*, in fact, said it out loud.

"Just a lucky guess. I mean, you're up here alone. I presumed there was either a complication in your career or a relationship issue."

"How'd you know I was alone?"

"Now, you're inquisitive. I like that." Mary lightly tapped Beth's knee. "I asked Alder."

"Why would you do that?"

Beth found it curious that such an unbridled woman as Mary would inquire about her. She was already trying not to notice the woman's astonishing attractiveness, not easy when Mary was sitting so close her body almost brushed Beth's with every movement.

Mary leaned unnervingly closer. "At the risk of sounding politically incorrect, I think you're very beautiful and I wondered who you were."

"I take it you're free to inquire about single women you meet?" Beth didn't want to be on the angry end of some hidden girlfriend.

Mary laughed. "I don't have a lover, if that's what you mean."

Beth felt herself loosen up a little. "That is what I mean. I don't want some jealous woman making me go running to Vicki and Candy for protection."

Mary placed her hand over Beth's. "Don't worry, I wouldn't let that happen to you."

She withdrew almost immediately, but the touch upon Beth's hand lingered. The caress had felt warm and soft. The odd paradox of this wild woman possessing such a calming touch made Beth's chest feel strange. She didn't know whether she was relieved, or unhappy that the touch had been so brief.

Recovering, she quickly countered, "You hardly know me."

"No one starts out knowing someone. We all start out as strangers, don't we?" Mary leaned in much too closely. "And the fun of starting out as strangers is that we get to become acquainted."

Beth sucked in a nervous breath, hoping Mary would move just a little further away. When she didn't, Beth observed, "Subtlety isn't listed anywhere on your résumé, is it?"

Mary grinned. "No, I guess it isn't." She ran her hand through her thick blond hair. "Would you like to hear my résumé?"

"Do tell." In fact, Beth did want to hear how this woman would describe herself. Was it possible that she hadn't thought of Stephanie in, oh, at least twenty minutes?

"Let's see. I'm Mary Walston. Thirty-three years old. Born in Malibu. Left home at seventeen. Fell in lust numerous times from seventeen to twenty-six. Discovered West Hollywood. Fell in love the same year. And ended up in San Francisco about three years ago."

"So, if I do the math, that leaves about four years unaccounted for."

"The lost years." Mary smirked. "During those dubious years I was venturesome, reckless, wild…cheeky. My mom always used that word. What else?"

"Unbridled?"

"Sure."

"Dauntless?"

"See, we're not such strangers after all." Mary smiled. "May I buy you a drink?"

"Would you be offended if I said no? I feel as though I'm some sort of target you happened to get a bead on tonight."

Mary looked at her, seemingly mulling it over, and then said calmly, "I understand your skepticism. Here comes this woman spouting on about your beauty. 'Bold' is another word I should have on that résumé. But I assure you there are many women here at this party that I don't know, and I don't care to know. And yes, you caught my attention this morning. I really hoped you'd come tonight and when I saw you, I wanted to tell you all this." Mary paused. "Beth, you're attractive and I wanted you to know that. How you respond to that is not anything I can control. And even if you tell me to get lost, I'll still be glad I told you."

Without thinking, Beth uttered, "Thank you."

Mary's candor was refreshing, but Beth still felt on guard. She could not allow any woman to get under her skin, and Mary was exactly the type who would. She was enchanting. Beth felt like she was in one of those classic black-and-white films where the gorgeous, bombshell woman bedazzles an awestruck gentleman. The man is blitzed by the woman's astonishing radiance and cannot believe he is the object of her attention. But this was not an old movie, it was here and now, and Beth was the unlikely object of Mary's attention.

She was not even sure if she was reading the signals correctly. The reason she'd ended up alone in San Francisco, in the middle of a party of strangers, was simple but painfully bona fide. She felt unwanted and undesirable, and had further contributed to her own plight by not sleeping, not eating, and generally not caring about herself. Thus, the puffy eyes, the gaunt look, and the wrinkled choice of clothes in the duffel bag.

Mary couldn't possibly be interested in her. She was too beautiful. Like Stephanie. And Stephanie hadn't wanted her. She couldn't trust Stephanie, and Mary probably fit into that category as well. Mary, Beth concluded, was toying with her.

From across the room, two women bellowed Mary's name and made their way through the crowd. Mary stood up and introduced the pair.

They hugged Mary and the younger of the two asked Beth, "Would you mind if we stole her for a second?" She already had Mary by the hand. "We've been looking for her all evening."

"Sure," Beth replied, thankful for the reprieve, yet a little deflated.

Before they walked out the front door, Mary leaned close and whispered, "I'll be back."

Beth seriously doubted it. She gave a noncommittal smile and let herself be sucked once more into the energy of the party. Eventually she ended up on the back porch, glad for the chance to catch her breath. She cracked open another beer but before she could lift the bottle to her lips, Keith grabbed her.

"I see that Mary thinks you're pretty interesting."

Beth decided that ignorance was the best response. "You do?"

Keith nodded. "Isn't she breathtaking?"

"She is." Literally.

"She's one popular woman," he said.

"I can't imagine she has too much trouble in the dating department." Beth knew her fishing was extremely obvious.

"That's an understatement." Keith guffawed. "She can't turn her head to sneeze without some luscious hottie handing over a tissue along with her apartment keys."

Figuring she'd already walked through the door Keith had opened, Beth asked, "Should I be careful of her?"

"Only if you decide to marry her." He jumped as an arm landed on his shoulder.

"Marry who?" Mary asked.

Beth's heart reacted noisily, thumping in her ears over the music coming from inside the house.

"Oh, no one, honey," Keith replied innocently.

Mary gave him a long look, then took Beth's hand. "Follow me."

"Now where are we going?"

The question only made it as far as the back of Mary's head. She was already leading Beth out of the kitchen and into the hallway between the staircase and the living room. Just as a man exited the bathroom in the hall, Mary ducked into the small space, pulling Beth with her.

"Why are we in the bathroom together?" Beth asked. "Do you need…assistance?"

"No." Mary laughed as she closed the door. "I didn't want to be interrupted again. I'm sorry my friends took me away from you. They wanted to show me their new car. But now I'm back."

Mary was doing that thing again, Beth thought. Her party posture was gone and she was expressing genuine sincerity. Their eyes locked and Beth found her mouth curling up to match Mary's smile. For a few seconds, she let herself bask in the delusion that she was the center of Mary's total and exclusive attention, then she called reality to mind. She thought about her first observation of Mary, when she was working the room at breakfast. No matter whom she talked to, she seemed to be very aware of everyone else in the kitchen, making sure everyone was greeted, acknowledged, and complimented. Perhaps she was making more of an effort with Beth because she was new here and not instantly impressed.

Mary's hand still held hers. The grip was warm and firm. Beth figured the little shocks she felt between their palms, like the ones you get from touching car doors in dry weather, were her imagination. But what Mary said next wasn't.

"Come here."

CHAPTER FIVE

Beth's breath escaped abruptly, leaving her instantly light-headed. Had they not been holding hands, her feet would have remained frozen, but Mary used their physical link to pull her closer. Her arms slid around Beth. They were face-to-face, inches from each other. Beth could smell the sweetness of beer on Mary's breath. All she could think about were Mary's lips. On hers. Automatically, she pushed Mary away.

There were at least five seconds of excruciating silence. Beth needed to say something, to explain her actions. But her mouth froze slightly opened. When she couldn't form any words, Mary offered some.

"Should I apologize?"

"I'm not sure." Which was true. Beth felt drawn to this woman, but she didn't want to play along. If Mary was playing.

"Do you feel the need to slap me?"

"No. It's just that I'm not used to kissing someone I hardly know." *And I'm not going to hand you a tissue and the keys to my apartment, either.*

"Hmm, that stranger stuff again."

Someone turned the door handle. Mary ignored the shuffling on the other side, but Beth saw an opportunity to escape. She wasn't comfortable hiding out in a bathroom with a woman she felt like kissing. She had enough problems.

"Mary, can we take a time-out, here?"

"The kind where I have to go sit in the corner?"

"No, the kind where I have to get some air."

Mary opened the door without a trace of embarrassment. The look she gave Beth was either brazenly confident or entirely guileless. Beth wished she could read her, but Mary was not as obvious as she seemed. She was one complex woman.

They went out to the back porch again. Most of the partygoers had gone inside to dance, leaving the wooden tables empty.

Mary scooped two beers out of a cooler and took the chair next to Beth's. "Just how long will it take before we're not strangers?"

"That depends."

Mary refused to echo Beth's flippant tone. Meeting her eyes, she asked, "On what? Whether we're honest with each other?"

Beth's neck prickled. Mary could see too much. "It's funny how that works. Or not." She couldn't stop the bitterness from leaking into her voice. "You think you know someone. After years. After living together. But it's no guarantee."

Because it wasn't about time, she thought; it was about trust.

Mary smiled at her so gently, tears rushed into Beth's eyes. "Tell me your last name, Beth."

"It's Standish."

"So even though you're on the lam from a woman, are you at least considering this a vacation of sorts?"

"I guess, in a way. I mean, I had planned on taking some

time out, just not like this. Not now." She looked at Mary. "Does that make any sense?"

"Yes. Sometimes we don't have the opportunity to pull out the travel brochures and select just the right vacation destination."

Beth nodded. "I registered for the race but had no hotel reservations. I didn't know where I was going to stay until I showed up here."

"Well, I think you made a good choice." The reply could simply have been a polite platitude, but Beth could tell that Mary really meant it.

"How long have you known Alder?"

"About three years, I guess." Mary seemed to spend a moment in happy recollection. "A friend of a friend dragged me to a party at the Coop one night. I must say, Alder's shindigs were a far cry from the hairspray-and-attitude parties I'd been used to."

"Hairspray and attitude?"

"That's L.A. Not all the L.A. parties are that way, but one is one too many."

"Say no more. It's nice in a crowd like this, where the music is great and no one is fighting or too drunk."

"Alder wouldn't stand for that and everyone knows it," Mary said.

"Would you call yourself a regular here at the Coop?"

"Not really, though I imagine living here would be quite fun. What's your opinion on that?" Mary looked genuinely interested.

"Well, I hardly count. I'm just a visitor, really. But I like being here. It's quiet but there's company when you need it. And Alder's like everyone's mom."

Mary nodded. "She always seems to have just the right thing to say at just the right time, doesn't she?"

A silly old expression came to Beth: *You ain't just whistling Dixie*. Smiling, she said, "Maybe she's psychic."

"Or maybe she just pays attention to life's lessons a little more than the rest of us impulsive slobs."

Beth laughed. "You may have a point there."

"What is it that you do that allows you to take unplanned time off?" Mary asked.

"I own a business doing home appraisals. The market is pretty flat. I just made the decision to go."

"You just walked away?"

"No." Beth was amused by the shock in Mary's face. Obviously she didn't seem like the kind of person who would simply abandon her career on a whim. Mary was right about that. "I left one of the women who work for me in charge."

"Will the business survive without you?"

"Oh, I'm sure. Candace is almost better at my job than I am." Beth tapped her beer bottle against Mary's. "So tell me, what do you set your alarm clock for every workday?"

"I'm a firefighter."

"Really?" Beth was impressed. "That must be intense."

Mary nodded. "I only work about ten days out of the month, but those ten days can be brutal."

"I can imagine. Tell me about a day in the life of a San Francisco firefighter."

Mary chuckled. "There's a lot of hurry up and wait. Every morning we have a meeting to discuss issues to do with the firehouse, the community, new laws, things like that. There's a workout room and a basketball hoop out back. I mostly keep myself busy."

"How often do you get called out?"

Mary took a swig of beer. "It varies. Most calls are for car accidents. We treat people at the scene and put out engine fires. House calls are usually routine. Smoke from overcooked dinners. Cats up trees."

She seemed to be avoiding talking about real emergencies, the dangerous ones. Curious, Beth asked, "What's it like when you get there and it's something really serious?"

Mary was silent for a moment, tapping her fingers on the table. "Not so long ago we got to this house in Noe Valley. Flames were shooting out of all the front windows and the neighbors were screaming that there were children inside. A babysitter came crawling out of the back door. She was dragging a toddler. She told us a five-year-old was still inside."

Dreading what was to come, Beth whispered, "Oh, no. Did you go inside?" She could picture Mary stumbling into a flaming building searching for a child.

"No, the baby was almost unconscious so I stayed with her to try to bring her around before the ambulance arrived. Two of the other guys went in. They found the little boy, but before they could get out there was another explosion."

"Oh, my God."

Mary nodded. "It could have been worse. They were right by a window, lifting the child out of his bunk bed. The explosion blew them out of the house. They landed on the grass not twenty feet from me."

"Did they survive?" Beth asked nervously. She wondered if this experience was the reason Mary had initially seemed reluctant to talk about the more frightening part of her job.

"Other than some good cuts and big bruises, they were okay. And the kids made it, too. Just a few nights in the hospital."

Beth shook her head. "Don't moments like that scare the hell out of you?"

"Yes, but it's the kind of fear that catapults you into action. You just react. There's no other choice."

Mary fell silent, seemingly lost in thought. Beth wondered where she'd gone. Was she reliving another call, where the victims hadn't been so lucky? Or was there some personal moment that was coming back? Whatever it was quickly vanished as Mary seemed to catch herself.

Raising her beer bottle, she said with humor that seemed forced, "Of course, it's easier to react when you're trained to do so. And I am at your service, ma'am."

Beth had no clue what caused her next statement, but it slipped out of her mouth. "Are you trained to put out every fire you see?"

A grin appeared instantly on Mary's face. "Only the kind I can control."

They stared at each other, not moving. Strangely, Beth was intensely excited but relaxed at the same time.

"Alder says you're up here to run the Half Marathon in two weeks." Mary said.

Beth nodded. "It was a good excuse to get out of L.A."

"Are you registered?"

"Yes, although the last half marathon I ran was in San Diego about five months ago, so I'm a little rusty."

"What's your PB?"

"My personal best? Usually only other runners use that term."

"I'm running in the Half this year as well. Helps me keep up with the fire hose pulling and stair climbing."

Beth wasn't sure how she felt knowing that Mary would be among the crowd of runners at the start line. "My PB was 2:03:29 two races ago. What about yours?"

"I'm just over two hours as well."

Great, they would even start in the same wave. "Are you running the first or second half?" Beth asked.

Runners could choose which half of the San Francisco Marathon course they wanted to run. The first half included an out and back across the Golden Gate Bridge. The second half was a longer race, but runners finished alongside those completing the full marathon.

"I registered for the first half," Mary said, dashing Beth's hope that they would be on different courses.

"The streets here are pretty hilly," Beth said. "I imagine my time will be slower."

"Well, I suppose it depends on how the weather affects you. It's usually pretty chilly out, and I find that it helps my time. I hate running in hot weather. Slows me down a lot."

The San Francisco Marathon was unique in that runners could aim for personal best times despite the race being held in summer. This wasn't important for Beth, but athletes were seeded by their times for the Boston Marathon. Those who planned to run both races tried to make a good showing in San Francisco.

"I'm not worried about my time," Beth said. "I just want to run, you know?"

"I do." Mary drew up her legs to sit cross-legged on the bench. "Sometimes just finishing is good enough for me."

Beth raised her beer. "Amen to that."

The evening moved stealthily toward late night. As they talked, the party raged around them. The back door opened and closed more times than Beth could count, but no one interrupted them. When the nippy night breezes began needling through their clothes, Mary asked Beth inside for a dance. The dance turned into another, and then a slow one.

Beth closed her eyes and let herself get lost in the swaying motion of their bodies. She couldn't keep her mind off the almost-kiss in the bathroom. She now half wished Mary had just tackled her and kissed her. As soon as she thought that, she scolded herself for getting carried away with fantasies about a wild woman who obviously knew her way around the ladies.

Mary whispered close to her ear, "This full body contact feels great."

Beth swore she heard Mary moan, but a crackle suddenly came from Jay's microphone. "Everyone ready? Let's all do the Teddy!" he bellowed as the next song began, Teddy Pendergrass singing "Close The Door."

A group of people moved to the middle of the dance floor and began gyrating and lip-synching to the song. One of the women reached out and grabbed Mary, pulling her into the group. Without much protest, Mary joined in so fluidly that Beth was enthralled by what she saw. Everyone knew the words perfectly, all the way down to the "uhhs" and "ahhhs." The group seemed to be doing some sort of sexual line dance, the kind where only a few people know the steps and everyone else watches and admires. They thrust their hips to punctuate each grunt, moving together in a pulsing erotic spectacle Beth thought was intended to be funny. She found it incredibly arousing, probably because the only person she was looking at was Mary.

She knew she was staring rather obviously, her whole focus concentrated on Mary's seductive moves. When Mary looked her way, she seemed to be singing to Beth, and only Beth. Her lips moved wetly and her eyes narrowed a little, languidly feasting. Beth knew she was not imagining the promise in their depths. Her gut reacted, tensing so sharply she wrapped her arms around her waist. The crowd was going berserk around her and she felt short of breath. People were too close and Mary's hips were grinding too suggestively to allow rational thought.

Beth started to back away but the crowd surged forward, quickly filling in the space around the singers as the song ended. As everyone converged, Mary ended up on the other side of the room. Beth stood frozen in her tracks, still taking in the erotic dance she'd just witnessed.

"Is she hot or what?" A woman nudged Beth's right shoulder and she recognized Maureen, a Coop resident she'd chatted with during the party preparations. "Mary's a wild woman. Don't let her scare you."

"Oh, I don't think 'scared' is the word I'd use."

"And do you care to share what *your* word would be?" Maureen was calmly teasing. "Or is don't let her *devour* you more apropos?"

Beth caught a glimpse of Mary between the bobbing heads of dancing guests. She was talking with a cute brunette, her smile just as alluring and her expression just as intent as it had been five minutes earlier, when Beth thought that look was just for her. Feeling foolish, she made excuses to Maureen and slid away to the kitchen. The table had been turned into shot glass central, with one of the Coop residents playing bartender.

Beth threw back an Alabama Slammer and chatted to a few people before escaping to her room. In the safe little retreat, she washed her face, brushed her teeth, and changed into a T-shirt and underwear before crawling into bed. The sheets felt crisp and cool against her body. She exhaled a big sigh and thought about the one thing that had dominated her mind all night.

Mary Walston.

The woman had cornered the market on sex appeal. Thinking back on her first impressions, Beth remembered thinking her "vainly cavalier." Now that she'd had the chance to talk to her, she decided to revise the description. The night, the conversations, her actions, all sketched out a new word. Confident. Tenaciously confident.

Beth shook her head. She had heard that somewhere out in the world there existed people who possessed that attribute. She could remember feeling something close to confidence herself, a long time ago.

The first time the knocking occurred, Beth thought it was part of the party commotion downstairs. When the noise persisted she got out of bed and opened the door to find Mary. Her warm olive green eyes trailed over Beth, making her self-conscious that she'd selected her most wrinkled T-shirt for bed and was only wearing a pair of skimpy panties beneath it.

"I didn't get to say good night to you." Mary leaned against the door. The expectancy in her gaze was unmistakable.

"That's sweet of you." Beth almost stepped aside to let her in, but she pictured Mary chatting with the brunette. No doubt she could take her pick and expected any woman she chose to fall gratefully into her arms.

"Maybe we should have stayed in the bathroom," Mary said. "I like talking to you without being interrupted. It's hard in a crowd. Someone always wants to take me away."

"You didn't seem unhappy about that." Beth was about to mention the brunette, but realized how jealous that would sound. She had no right to guilt-trip Mary.

"I know," Mary conceded. "I get caught up."

For the second time in ten seconds, Beth wanted to invite her in. The idea startled her more than it excited her, and she blurted out, "I've got to get some sleep."

She realized, with alarm, how lame that sounded. All she wanted to do was pull Mary inside and re-create that moment in the bathroom, but this time with a different outcome. With horror, she recognized how close she was to making the kind of careless decision women on the rebound made. What she really needed to do was end the conversation as quickly and impersonally as possible.

"Thank you for a nice evening, Mary."

Mary stared into her eyes and it was obvious that she could read Beth's true thoughts. She acknowledged the polite brush-off with a knowing smile and a nod of regret. "Sleep well. I guess I'll see you later…sometime."

Beth forced a smile. Even though Mary was the one being adjourned, it was Beth who felt disarmingly awkward.

Chapter Six

Most of Sunday, after helping the household clean up from the party, Beth sat in a beach chair out in the backyard among the flowers, head back, face in the sun. She couldn't keep her mind off Mary. It felt strange thinking about Mary's energy, her body, and how she felt when they were dancing. Mary had come into her life not more than twenty-four hours before and it seemed crazy that she had now invaded so many brain cells.

"You and Mary got along famously, I see."

Beth looked up with a start. Alder was standing over her with a tall glass of iced tea. Thanking her, Beth accepted the drink and replied, "She's a wild woman."

"That's an understatement." Alder pulled up another chair and sat down.

"I had a great time last night. I wasn't expecting to, but you know how to put on a good party." Beth thought of the music and the dancers. Remembering her last conversation with Alder, she ventured, "You said last night that it's not 'running away' as long as people deal with why they leave."

"That sounds like something I would say," Alder conceded.

Beth paused over a sip of the refreshing tea. "It's my ex.

She cheated on me, then dumped me. I couldn't stand the whole scene and how it was making me feel, so I left. But I've been thinking I need to talk to her. Maybe. Oh, I don't know."

"She made her decisions," Alder said. "It's not the two of you that need to talk. You need to talk to yourself."

Beth grimaced. "I feel like I've been doing a lot of that."

"But you're stuck thinking the same things over and over?"

"Pretty much."

"Then it's time to ask yourself the questions you need to ask and trust that the answers will come, no matter where you are. Because the answers are out there." Alder smiled. "Somewhere in your healthy mind."

"Healthy?"

"Yes, it's that state of being just after insanity."

Beth let her fingers drift, making circles in the condensation on her glass. The pale liquid quivered, rippling in wavy rings. "Alder," Beth wasn't sure she should inquire, but went ahead, "is that Mary's MO? I mean, being forward with women she hardly knows?"

Alder looked up to the sky and laughed. "Mary is the freest spirit I know. She loves life and let's everyone know it. As for her modus operandi with women, why not ask her yourself?" There was a teasing twinkle in her eyes.

"Oh, sure. I want to be *that* obvious." Beth pondered her first impressions of Mary. Seizing life like it was the lone, single buoy in a stormy sea. "It's like she has no fears."

"But she does," Alder corrected.

"What fears could she possibly have?"

"That's hers to tell." Alder got up slowly, stretching her back as she went to get some trash bags. She returned a minute later with a mysterious smile on her face. "The door. It's for you."

As Beth sprang from her chair, Mary emerged from the house and waved as she advanced toward them. "I've come a-callin'."

"Oh, brother." Alder shook her head as she walked away.

Smiling over the mock repudiation, Beth turned to Mary. "You have, have you?"

"Yes, I have. I'd like to ask you something."

"What?" At once, Beth felt a slight panic, afraid that Mary might ask her out on a date. Strangely, she was also afraid that she wouldn't.

"I have both five- and ten-mile routes that I run, and I was wondering if you'd like to train with me for the race. It helps me when I run with other people. Takes my mind off the running."

Beth hesitated. Running alone was therapeutic for her. Having a running partner hadn't even been a slight notion. But then again, Mary's route would already be laid out and she wouldn't get lost or find herself in a less-than-desirable neighborhood. She had briefly considered signing up for the official San Francisco Marathon training program or one of the intensive boot camps, but she didn't have endless time to spend. All she needed was to be fit enough to complete the race with an average time. Perhaps running with a partner would help her motivation level.

"I'd like that," she finally said.

"Great. I'm going out later this afternoon, say five o'clock. Care to start then?"

"No time like the present. Where shall I meet you?"

"We can start from here. Given that the race is in two weeks, I imagine you're running some combinations."

Mary nodded. "Alternating running and resting, yes. Three, six, and then nine or ten miles this week."

"And an easy week leading up to the race?"

Beth nodded. "Two or three miles, then rest a day, like that."

"Me, too. We're very close in our training schedules. It's perfect, then. I'll come by at five, okay?"

"I'll be here." Beth indicated the chair Alder had vacated. "Want to hang out for a while?"

She tried not to be disappointed when Mary shook her head and said she had things to do. Watching her saunter back toward the house, Beth did as Alder had suggested and asked herself a question, the one she'd been trying to avoid ever since she first set eyes on Mary Walston.

Am I going to sleep with this woman?

"Man, I'm feeling it in my calves," Beth said when they were on their third mile.

"Need to stop? We can take a shortcut and get back to the Coop in another mile or so."

"Let's do that. We can either take a rest day tomorrow or go just a few."

The early evening was mildly foggy and crisp, filling Beth's lungs with fresh, salty air. They'd run through the Castro and through part of Golden Gate Park and were on their way back.

"Where do you run in L.A.?" Mary asked when they began to pick up speed again.

"Through the neighborhoods in Long Beach, where I live."

"Do you like living there?"

Beth was not quite sure any more. "I did."

"Care to elaborate?"

"My ex lives there."

"Ah, *the woman*," Mary noted. "The reason you had to leave."

"Yes. We broke up a few months ago and it hasn't been easy." Beth wiped some sweat from her brow. "In a city as big as L.A., if I tried to find her, I never would. But when I'd rather not see her, she's at the gas station, or the grocery store, or the dry cleaners. Without fail."

"Why is that?" Mary mused as they skirted a couple and their dog.

"The second law of thermodynamics, I suppose."

Mary laughed. "Hey, I just put out fires. What the hell does that mean?"

"All organization tends toward disorganization."

They ran a half a block further before Mary said, "You mean, when you want a relationship, it gets screwed up. Then, when you want someone to be out of your life, they're always around?"

"Damn skippy."

"How many laws of thermodynamics are there?" Mary asked.

"Three, I think."

"And you know this how?"

"Lots of time on my hands and too many encyclopedias lying around when I was a kid." Beth hoped she wasn't making herself sound boring from birth.

"No tree houses and mud pies?"

"Not in my family. Too ghastly for a little girl, as my mother would say."

"Encyclopedias and thermodynamic laws sound pretty ghastly to me."

"Hey, that's my childhood you're talking about." Beth playfully pushed Mary enough to cause her to stagger, and then charged ahead.

A stinging pain shot through her left calf muscle but she puckishly dashed ahead. Mary chased after her and caught up to her within a block. Throwing her arms around Beth, she swung her around. The momentum of their speed caused them to pirouette twice and they stumbled to a stop, winded and laughing raucously.

"Don't tell me you were a bookworm and now you're sensitive about it," Mary gasped, still wrapped around her.

The heat from her body made Beth's knees weaken and she felt a flush rise from her chest to her hairline. Standing that close, she could see little speckles of brown in Mary's eyes and feel Mary's warm breath as she puffed from the recent exertion. Mary's smile was as inviting as it was sultry. Beth could have kissed her right then, just like in the bathroom at the party.

Determined not to succumb, she said, "I can't help it that my mom was a curmudgeon." She moved away from Mary. "Anyway, better smart than dirty."

"I think you've got that backward."

"Maybe." But Beth thought Mary might be right. She just didn't want to think about that now, not with Mary looking so incredibly sexy. Her initial thoughts about Mary as vainly cavalier were being challenged. *She's still trouble*, she told herself and looked at her watch. "We have another two miles to go."

"Okay. But no more sprints. I'm almost out of gas here."

"Agreed."

They slowed their pace a little on a steep downhill slope.

"How did you get into the real estate business?" Mary asked.

"After college I went to work for a grocery store," Beth replied. "Just to pay the bills. I knew I'd never enjoy corporate America, so I decided to take advantage of the booming real estate market so I could work for myself and not deal with water cooler politics. I got licensed in appraising houses."

"Did it work out the way you imagined?"

"Almost. I now have a staff of three. Two appraisers and a secretary who manages the office, so in a way, I've created my own little corporation. Except that I refuse to order a water cooler."

They made their final turn and finished their run in front of the Coop. Beth was tired, but the sights along the way and the conversation she'd enjoyed with Mary had made the run an entirely different experience. She felt energized and clearheaded and was surprised at how loose her shoulders were. Months of tension seemed to have drained out through her fingertips as she ran.

She groaned through her first stretches. "I'm going to have to soak my calves tonight."

"I know." Mary laughed. "When I first moved here, I thought I'd have to become a mountain goat to navigate these hills. They can be brutal."

She reached down to touch her toes. Her sinewy thighs glistened with sweat from her recent exertion, and Beth was mesmerized at the alluring droplets that followed the curves of her quadriceps.

"What? Do I have gum on my ass?"

Beth jolted out of her reverie to find Mary looking at her from her bent-over position. "I was just...staring off into space."

Mary wasn't taken in by the feeble explanation. "You were looking at my ass."

"I was not."

"You were."

Beth sighed. "I was."

Mary chuckled as Beth started toward the front steps.

She'd only taken a few paces when her heel struck the ground and her leg muscles refused to function. She cried out in pain.

"What's the matter?" Mary leaned over toward her but Beth twisted away.

"Leg. Cramp," was all she could get out.

Mary knelt down. Taking Beth's leg, she lifted it onto her knee. As Beth writhed and groaned in agony, Mary dug her thumbs into Beth's calf muscle.

"Breathe. As deeply as you can." She continued to work out the knot as Beth gasped out deep breaths between cries and curses. "You sound like my uncle's fifty-seven Buick right before it finally broke down for good."

"Not funny." Somewhere in the back of her brain, Beth knew she should be seriously considering the fact that Mary was touching her, let alone whether she should even be touching her, but she was in too much pain to do anything but whimper.

She closed her eyes and focused on the massage, willing her calf to relax. Knowing that it was Mary's hands that worked her muscle certainly made the spasm feel better, but she was also self-consciously aware that her face had been twisted up into what must be a pretty hideous expression. Under different circumstances, she might lay her head back and smile a satisfied smile. But under different circumstances, would she let Mary massage her leg?

Finally, the kneading did the trick and the pain subsided. Beth blew out a mouthful of air. Now that she was almost free of the cramp, she took a guilty moment to just feel Mary's hands. They were strong and warm, and the slow rhythm of her strokes made Beth close her eyes and drift with the feeling. She knew she should tell Mary that she'd eliminated the cramp, but her hands felt so good.

"It's feeling okay now," she said reluctantly. "Thank you, Mary."

When Mary shifted to move Beth's leg off her knee, Beth stopped her, covering Mary's hand with her own. As they locked eyes, Beth knew Mary was probably wondering what this gesture meant. She wasn't even sure herself, since she hadn't known that she was going to do it until her hand closed over Mary's. But it had seemed as natural and automatic as hugging one's arms around one's body upon walking into a freezing wind.

What should she tell her? What was the truth? Did she want Mary to get going? Yes. Was she still apprehensive about her? Another yes. She squeezed the hands that felt so good around her leg.

"That really helped," she said, convinced that the feeling of falling into Mary's green eyes was dangerous.

She released Mary's hand and they stepped back from each other. Mary gave her a brief, uncertain look then adopted an impersonal tone. "Were you hydrated, Beth?"

"I was. I think I'm just not used to the hills."

"Well, I don't have to tell you to make sure you continue to hydrate and get some potassium in you." Mary seemed intent on some moss near her shoe, scuffing it with her toe. "Thank you for the run. Let me know if you'd like to go again tomorrow." She paused. "You know, your calves and all."

"I need to, actually, regardless of what my calves might complain about."

"I'm off for the next few days," Mary said. "We should probably only do a couple of miles tomorrow."

"Great." Beth wanted to ask Mary in but she felt awkward, and by the time she found the right words, Mary had already taken off.

Watching her jog slowly down the street, Beth hoped she didn't turn around and catch her staring. She had a bad feeling her face had pathetic lust written all over it. When Mary glanced back over her shoulder, Beth quickly ducked inside the door, mumbling, "Damn."

"Bad run?" Alder was sitting on the couch in the front room reading a magazine.

"No. It was great."

"And that's cause to swear?"

Beth plopped down in an easy chair. "Yeah."

Alder closed the magazine and got up. "Follow me."

They adjourned to the kitchen. Beth sat at the table while Alder turned on the coffee pot.

"So tell me about the bad movie," Alder said.

"What?"

"I have a feeling it's related to your swearing. You said at the party that your home situation was like a bad movie and that you'd only talk about it over coffee."

"Fair enough." Beth decided she was ready for this, and even if she wasn't, it would probably help to tell someone a few of the details. "It's a fairly simple story. We moved in together after dating for five months. For a while it worked, then I found out that she'd been having an affair with a woman she worked with. That had been going on for a while. And to make matters worse, she dumped me."

Alder poured their coffee and sat down, pushing a mug toward Beth. "How'd that come about?"

Beth shook her head. "I was an idiot. I ranted and raved about the affair. My ex said she had to think about things, which meant she wanted time to decide between me and the other woman."

"And?"

Beth took a long swallow of java. "I told her to think about it somewhere else. And she did."

"At the other woman's house?"

"Yup." Beth sighed heavily. "She sent me a text message a week later telling me that I was yesterday's news."

"And now you're kicking yourself for being with her and for getting hurt."

"Of course." Beth dropped her head, running her hands through her hair. "I thought it couldn't happen. I'm not a kid. She was perfect for me, and I thought I was a reasonable judge of character. It's hard when you can't trust your own judgment anymore."

"Maybe you moved in together too quickly. Maybe you never got to really know her the way you should have."

"I'd say that's a very astute conjecture."

"But it's now in your past," Alder said. "And I have faith that you've learned from it."

"I will as soon as I can get her out of my head."

"So, you're hurt because she cheated on you. But you still want her?"

"I don't know. She just threw away three years. When I think about that, I want to call her because that time mattered. But knowing she lied to me for six months while she slept with someone else makes me sick."

"She couldn't have been that perfect."

The slam of a door upstairs followed by an uproarious squeal silenced Alder. Gina came running into the kitchen being chased by Diane, who was clutching a handful of ice. Alder ignored them, taking a moment to sip her coffee. As they lunged at each other around the table, Beth hunkered down, attempting to stay out of the line of fire.

"If I promise to give you a backrub, will you stop with the ice?" Gina's eyes darted toward the door.

"Striking bargains is the sign of a guilty person." Diane held the ice up higher.

"Take it outside, lovebirds," Alder said blandly.

Gina bolted for the door, Diane on her heels.

"There will now be three hours of silence," Alder said.

Just then, Keith's high-pitched holler pierced melodically through the heavy air. He was headed toward the kitchen.

Alder yelled, "What'd you buy for dinner?"

"Nothing." He appeared from around the corner. "Take me to dinner?"

"Like we're your slave girls," Alder said. "Go pound sand."

"Oh come on, Alder. My car's broken and I'm feeling like Mexican tonight. Would someone give me a ride? Please?"

"That's more like it, young man." She got up and patted Beth on the shoulder. "Don't look so glum. Remember, you're out of that relationship." She grabbed her keys. "Care to come along?"

Beth declined with a smile. After they'd traipsed off, she stared out the kitchen window, watching the sun go down. A strong wind blew the trees in the backyard, rattling the leaves and making the branches creak. Vignettes of her life with Stephanie pitched back and forth, much like the trees, and Beth resolutely endured the assault. This time, however, the usual tears didn't come. She seemed to be detached, looking back from a safe distance. The view offered greater clarity and she saw something she'd never seen before.

Even before the fighting and the cheating, Stephanie didn't love her.

CHAPTER SEVEN

Monday morning was socked in with fog. Beth rose around seven, thinking it was much earlier. She padded over to her bedroom window and was immediately struck by how thick the air had become. If God had decided to be chef that day, his plate du jour was obviously gray consommé. Though the weather was unusually dense, even for San Francisco, it hardly slowed anyone down. Monday morning was business as usual for the Coop's residents. The only ones who hadn't shoved off to work by seven thirty were Alder and Maureen. They were finishing breakfast when Beth strolled downstairs.

"Good morning, ladies." Beth poured herself a cup of coffee.

"Beth, you look chipper. Did you take an obscenely early run or are you just adoring being with us?" Alder flipped through the pages of a newspaper.

Smiling, Beth sat down at the table. "Mary's coming by at ten for a run."

"I wish I could do the same today." Maureen crunched on a piece of toast. "I need to get bikini-ready for my vacation to Mazatlan."

"Mazatlan? That sounds like a great time."

"Yes, and she'd better bring back some beer, like she promised," Alder said. "Bohemia. Now, that's a beer."

Beth had tried a few Mexican lagers but she'd never heard of the beer Alder was talking about.

"It's stronger than Dos Equis and Negra Modelo," Maureen said. "It's pretty good and hard to get, this side of the border."

"That ought to charge up the next Coop party," Alder predicated.

Beth laughed. "Like the Coop parties need sparking up. I've only been to one and it was a doozy."

Alder shot her a sly glance. "It's all in the company, right, Beth?"

"Yeah, uh-huh." Maureen chimed in. "There were so many sparks between you and Mary, I told Alder to turn off the gas to the stove."

Alder's booming laugh rattled the table. Beth felt herself turning red but couldn't help but join in. "You could embarrass a girl."

Alder pointed to Beth's face. "Looks like we already did."

Maureen patted Beth's arm. "We're just joking with you because we really like Mary. And we can tell she thinks you're a hottie."

Beth felt a slight swirl in her chest. "She's pretty… amazing, but probably half the people in the city think that."

"More than half," Alder corrected.

Maureen downed the rest of her coffee. "What's that got to do with the price of condoms in San Francisco?"

"And more to the point, what are you going to do about it?" Alder asked playfully.

"Probably nothing." Beth shrugged. "I've been pretty morose lately. Lord knows, that's not too alluring."

"You stop that," Alder scolded. "She sees what we all see, a bright and beautiful woman."

"Just look in the mirror," Maureen said. "Besides, all you need to do is enjoy yourself while you're here. You're on vacation."

Beth raised her coffee cup to Maureen. "Speaking of vacations, may yours arrive swiftly and pass slowly."

"You said a mouthful, sister," Maureen rejoined. "Oh, Lord. Look at the time. I'll be late for work." With that, she jumped up and placed her coffee cup in the sink. "Have a great day," she called out as she headed for the front door.

"Are you working today, Alder?" Beth asked.

The older woman nodded. "Yes. It's the American dream. Buy a house bigger than your budget will allow and spend years in debt."

"But what a great place to be indebted to."

"This is true. I can honestly say that I believe I have come home."

A wonderful belief, Beth thought, a belief that eluded her at the moment.

"So." Alder nudged her. "What's on the agenda for later this afternoon?"

"Actually, I haven't even given it a thought. Get lost somewhere, maybe."

"There are lots of places to get lost around here."

"Yeah?"

Alder nodded. "And in my experience, the more you try to get lost, the faster you end up finding yourself."

"If you keep getting all philosophical on me, I might have to stop feeling sorry for myself," Beth said wryly.

"Don't you hate when other people won't join the pity party?"

Beth feigned shock. "Are you suggesting one person crying in her beer is enough?"

Alder offered one of her sage smiles. "Did you notice your eyes aren't puffy today?"

As a matter of fact, Beth had. "I guess I forgot to cry myself to sleep."

"So it seems." Alder left the table with a look of satisfaction. A few minutes later the front door clicked shut behind her.

Alone in the house, Beth read the newspaper, then climbed upstairs to shower and change into her running clothes. As she bent to tighten her shoes, a lone image came to mind of Mary stretching on the front steps after their run the day before. Beth laughed out loud thinking about being caught looking at Mary's alluring legs. Mary's face was beautiful. Her cheeks were pink from the physical exertion and her eyes twinkled with playfulness.

Beth stroked the calf Mary had massaged. It was slightly tender, and she rubbed her muscle briskly to warm it. She had thought about skipping the run, but she didn't want to spend the whole day alone. More than that, she didn't want to miss the chance to see Mary. She was already downstairs when Mary knocked, and she almost fell out of the door into her arms.

"You ready?" Mary asked.

"Absolutely."

The weather was perfect. Though the air was a little chilly, the sun was shining, which would keep Beth's hands and ears from getting too cold.

Mary walked with Beth out to the street, where they stopped to stretch. "How are the calves?"

"I soaked them last night. They're pretty tight now, but if we start out slowly, they should warm up."

She stretched her legs and thought of their last run. The conversation had been easy and comfortable, even when they touched on a few sensitive areas. She hadn't enjoyed herself so much for a long time. She grinned remembering how she dashed off, with Mary chasing and finally catching her. And later, when Mary had massaged the horrible cramp out of her calf, she'd almost wallowed in the feel of those hands kneading her muscles.

For a new, and not to mention dangerous friend, Mary sure touched her a lot, and Beth did nothing to stop her. She was getting to like Mary even though she knew she should be cautious. Beth avoided the tempting sight of Mary's long, sleek legs just inches away. It would be all too easy to brush against them accidentally, then linger for more. Mary certainly wasn't averse to physical contact. She was seeking it out, if Beth was any judge of body language. She turned her attention to her watch, trying to steer her thoughts on track. She had a race to train for and would enjoy her time with her new running partner, but she'd also keep her guard up.

For the first mile, they ran a leisurely ten-and-a-half-minute pace, taking roughly a minute off their previous time. They didn't push any harder. They needed to follow a disciplined training schedule so they would be fit for the distance without overtraining and hurting their performance on race day. Beth concentrated on her breathing. She could feel the tension beginning to ease in her calves. The rigidity in her muscles felt like pebbles, rather than the boulders she'd woken up with.

"That was a first-rate cramp last night," Mary remarked as they worked into a relaxed stride.

"Muscle pain sucks."

"All pain sucks."

Beth wondered what pain Mary had endured in her life. "All pain?"

"Most pain."

"Physical or emotional?"

Mary paused. "Physical and emotional."

Beth thought about Mary's life and the four lost years. She wondered about the fear that didn't seem to show itself, but that Alder had referred to. Was it due to a bad breakup? Was there a family crisis or loss? Beth couldn't imagine a confident person like Mary haunted by inner doubts.

"Have you ever had your heart broken, Mary?"

Mary was silent for a long moment. Her eyes seemed to focus on something distant. There was a sadness etched across her face, making her expression recoil as if she were wincing from a punch thrown to her stomach. Beth was just about to apologize for asking such a personal question when Mary finally spoke.

"Yes." Her face relaxed but she didn't elaborate. A slow smile erased the sadness. "How are you doing?"

"It just aches a little."

"That wasn't what I meant."

Focusing on the thuds of their feet striking the earth in tandem, Beth let the comment register. The painful lump in the center of her chest no longer constrained her breathing. Over the past three days, she'd actually had periods of longer than an hour when she didn't think about Stephanie once.

She glanced sideways. "I'm doing better. Thank you for asking."

A gust of wind caught Mary's hair, lifting tendrils of shimmering blond. Her broad smile and her bright eyes warmed Beth to her core. Mary was looking at her the way Beth sometimes looked at beautiful flowers, filled with awe that nature could render such perfection with seemingly careless abandon.

They ran in silence for a long while, and at first, Beth worried that she'd upset Mary by asking about the broken heart. She'd seen a change in her but couldn't read the reason for it.

Eventually, after they'd turned toward home, she said, "I didn't intend to be inquisitive."

Mary slowed a little. "Everyone has their tender spots. If we don't ask each other questions, we won't know what they are."

"Perhaps you'll tell me about yours sometime."

"If you really want to know," Mary replied.

"I do."

It was the truth. Beth wanted to learn who this woman was beneath her compelling charm. The urge made her anxious. The timing was all wrong. Yet she couldn't dismiss the irrational sense that, since the moment she'd left L.A., nothing was entirely accidental. If she hadn't found herself standing in front of the Coop three days ago, she would not have met Mary. And, right now, she would have been in a hotel on Fisherman's Wharf, planning for her race alone and wondering what she was going to do when she returned to L.A.

"Beth?" Mary's voice broke in on her racing thoughts after a while.

Turning toward her, Beth smiled. "Yes?"

"We ran past the Coop."

In disbelief, Beth slowed down and took in her surroundings. She glanced back, and sure enough, the Coop was a block behind them. "Oh."

They stopped and held their sides, laughing as they caught their breath. After a few stretches, they walked back, occasionally exchanging glances that left a lot unsaid.

When they reached the house, Beth asked, "Would you like to run again tomorrow?"

Mary replied just as impersonally, "You're my running partner until the race, but tomorrow's a rest day."

"You're right."

As they spoke, the air between them seemed hazy with electricity. Beth knew she wasn't imagining the heat in Mary's eyes. Yet they continued making arrangements like neither of them was aware of the tension.

"I'll pick you up at ten," Mary said. "Bring a light jacket or sweatshirt, okay?"

"I thought we weren't running."

"We're not. We're walking."

"Where are we walking?"

"Ocean Beach. You'll love it."

"I'm looking forward to it," Beth said, really meaning it.

"Get some potassium in you, okay?" Mary lifted one hand in a friendly wave as she jogged off.

Beth stared after her for a few seconds, dismayed that she hadn't stayed to chat. Then she told herself it was probably fortunate. Where Mary was concerned, she was liable to made decisions she might later regret. Beth decided a new rule was necessary. *Avoid temptation.*

CHAPTER EIGHT

Beth showered, letting the hot water soak into her calf for quite a while. Around four o'clock she threw on her jacket and ventured outside.

The air had turned much colder. The fog that cloaked the city had trapped the frigid ocean air underneath. The wind picked up the sea's moisture and carried it inland, leaving a cool dampness on Beth's face. As she walked back toward the Castro, a nucleus she felt comfortably drawn to, she took out her cell phone and called Candace.

"I told you not to call," her employee said. "There's nothing I can't handle right now."

"Hello to you, too," Beth teased. Candace had been adamant about her taking a break.

"Are you okay?" Candace asked.

"Actually, I am. I know this was a crazy impulse, but I'm glad to be here."

"You've earned it and you can sure use the change of scenery," Candace said. "Relax and enjoy yourself,"

"I'm trying to, but part of me thinks I shouldn't have left. What if we get a barrage of work and have to turn them around quickly?"

"I seriously doubt it, in this market." Candace laughed.

"Listen, you took care of things when my mother got sick last year, and I can do the same now. Don't fret over this one, Beth. I know you needed to get away and I've got you covered. Just get your mind off L.A. for a while, would you?"

Beth sighed. "Thanks, Candace. I'll call you after the race."

Candace wished her luck and told her again not to worry. Laughing Beth ended the call and slid the phone back into her jacket.

As she strolled toward Castro Street, Candace's advice began to permeate her brain. She was here to get her mind off L.A. and calling the business every day was an unnecessary reminder of all that awaited her when she returned. Of course, she could erase the pressures of work for a while. Stephanie, she couldn't. There had been deceit and lies, and her life had been torn apart. That horrible cringing feeling came back again as she reached the main drag, and her stomach bunched. She found refuge in a café, sitting at a mahogany table and staring at the menu. She was relieved when the waitress paid her immediate caffeinated attention. Hopefully a chicken crepe would fend off her stomach knots.

Beth shook off the cold as she sipped her coffee and let her gaze wander around the room. She wasn't the only person sitting alone, but she felt conspicuous. Everyone else looked content, reading newspapers or pecking at their BlackBerry smartphones. She took inventory of the day and time. Monday afternoon. Stephanie would be at work or maybe she'd taken the day off. Either way, she'd probably awoken in the arms of that other woman. On the side of the bed that had belonged to Beth. A side that was supposed to be hers as they grew old together.

Didn't Stephanie know how much Beth loved her? And that Beth would have done anything for her? No, she didn't.

Or worse yet, she didn't care. All she cared about was bedding some other woman and throwing away three years.

"Here, I thought you might like another one." The waitress had returned and was holding out a napkin.

Beth looked down to find hers shredded. Feeling completely foolish, all she could muster was, "Thanks."

"Women." The waitress guessed her plight. "You can't live with 'em and you can't shoot 'em."

Well, Beth thought, there was nothing she could do about it now. She'd left L.A. in order to get the breakup off her mind, and so far she'd been able to keep her most negative thoughts at bay. She sliced into her crepe and concentrated on doing just that. She was far from home, and the cool blast of air that blew her way every time the door opened reminded her of that fact. So it shouldn't be too hard to let go of all that L.A. represented, and start anew. By the time she went back, she wanted to feel more interested in the future than the past.

She looked around the restaurant once more. It was elegantly decorated but still retained a neighborhood feel. She liked the village atmosphere of the Castro. Even with the crowds of tourists, the neighborhood felt laid back and friendly. She could be happy living in a place like this, not that relocating was likely. Still, Beth welcomed the fleeting thought. Lately, her life had felt devoid of possibility. She'd been trapped by her sorrow and attachment, unable to move forward. That had changed.

Not only was her journey to San Francisco physical, it was also emotional. She'd always known that, but she'd had low expectations. Now it was as though a door had opened and all she had to do was walk through it. She was halfway there already, wanting to explore what lay on the other side. All she needed was a little more confidence.

After eating, Beth retrieved her Mercedes. She wasn't

ready to go back to the Coop, so she took a drive around the city. She flipped around the radio dial until she found a station that played soft rock. Right after two great '80s songs, Mariah Carey's "Always Be My Baby" came on. That was *their* song. She could almost feel Stephanie's body against hers as they danced to it. Her stomach twisted and she cursed out loud. What a crock of shit.

She had to get Stephanie off her mind. She drove everywhere she could think of in an attempt to shake off the tentacles of her ex that wrapped incessantly around her brain. She spent some time in the Exploratorium watching the children play. She listened to their untroubled laughter as they manipulated each interactive science exhibit. A while later, she stopped off in Chinatown to buy freshly baked fortune cookies. She ate seven of them, not reading any of the fortunes. A giggle even managed to surface when a street juggler entertained some tourists at Fisherman's Wharf.

She'd covered a lot of the northern portion of the city, and as she drove back to the Coop, she realized that her day had been punctuated by moments of relaxation and lighter thoughts. Stephanie had actually started to fade again. Like a dirt stain held under running water, the ugly spot was beginning to release its grip. Well, maybe one that might need a little more elbow grease.

After parking near the Coop, Beth let herself in, climbed the stairs to her room, and plopped down on the bed. If she could completely exorcize Stephanie from her brain, maybe she could get back to some semblance of a normal life. Spending time with Mary would help that process. But, then again, maybe it would snarl everything up.

She couldn't argue with the fact that Mary was a rather enjoyable distraction from her life in L.A. But she was becoming more than that. She was charming and straightforward in a way that was entirely refreshing. And she sure wasn't anything like Stephanie. Mary told people exactly what she thought without vagueness or trepidation. She had an endless exuberance and approached people and situations with such genuineness and self-assurance that Beth couldn't help but be drawn to her.

She was pleasantly surprised at her growing attraction to the firefighter. She wondered what it would be like to kiss Mary. She was sure her lips would be soft and inviting. She closed her eyes and could almost feel the warmth of Mary's face in her hands and the electrifying thrust of her tongue, assuredly talented and sexy.

Beth played it out in her mind. As they kissed, she'd reach down to caress Mary's leg, breathing in the distinctive mixture of sweat and salt air as she ran one hand over taut, lithe muscles. Mary would pull away from the kiss, her lips wet and silky. Her expression would be full of longing. Beth would become light-headed from the smoldering look, falling into eyes that would signal a shared desire. She would claim Mary's mouth again, giving in to the essential and primitive need for more, just as she would gulp for air if trapped in a ferocious whirlpool.

Their mouths would meld, as would their bodies, pushing into each other. Mary would reach behind Beth, clutching her cheeks through her running shorts, pinning them together in heated embrace. The pressure would make her squirm and she would feel Mary's excitement rise to match her own. She would bite and tug at Mary's lower lip. The kissing, the moist and sultry heat, and the amazingly slow but hit-the-mark grinding would be too much. Mary wouldn't let go, claiming Beth as hers in that moment.

Beth opened her eyes. Where had that come from? Not so much the kissing, because she'd imagined that from the first moment Mary had dragged her into the bathroom at the party on Saturday night. But imagining Mary gripping her ass in such a provocative way? Stephanie had never done anything like that, and Beth couldn't remember ever wanting her to.

In the beginning, their relationship had been like any honeymoon, full of silly laughter, rumpled bed sheets, sexy whispers, and ravenous gazes. Stephanie was stable and collected. She was as successful as Beth. They had many mutual friends and enjoyed a committed lovership in a desirable, established neighborhood. There were no surprises and no tension. Everyone viewed their relationship as a model of lesbian success, and they went about life as any couple would, with honest work, errand running, home remodeling, pleasant vacations, and social gatherings. Everything had been fine until the last three months of their relationship, when Stephanie suddenly became sullen, casting a morose cloud that obscured the picture of a happy relationship. They began to fight and even worse, not talk at all.

Beth had clung to the relationship, trying frantically to repair a break she couldn't even see. She remained devoted to Stephanie, even as the emotional gap between them widened. Their relationship had been so strong for so long that Beth refused to accept that it could just disintegrate. And then one evening, when she returned from work, she found Stephanie sitting in the dark, very drunk and infuriated. She spat angry accusations at Beth, most of which she didn't understand, but all of which were claims that Beth was an incompetent lover who bored her stiff. Stephanie said she loathed waking up with her because she wasn't exciting anymore. She blamed Beth for causing her recent depression.

Beth could have been slapped and it wouldn't have dazed her as much. Stephanie was the one who'd withdrawn and shut down. She was the one who seemed to be throwing their relationship away. And Beth wasn't going to give the alcohol any credit for the outburst. The ensuing discussion echoed in her mind.

"Since when did I become responsible for your depression?" she'd demanded.

"Do you see anyone else in this house?" Stephanie retorted sarcastically.

"Well yes, actually. You."

"I'm not happy. Can't you see that? Living with you is making me…suffocate."

"You're not making any sense, Steph."

"Then maybe this will." Stephanie's eyes had grown black. "I'm not in love with you anymore. And I had to get drunk to say that."

Shock slapped Beth so hard, it drove her back a step. She couldn't reply, and what followed was an agonizing isolation she didn't think she could survive. Stephanie had refused to talk to her about that night's conversation or much of anything else. Beth tried to reason with her, asking her to think about their relationship and what they'd built together. She asked her to agree to couples counseling, and in one of the first sessions, Stephanie revealed her reasons for getting into their relationship. She'd been attracted to Beth's stability. She'd reasoned that if she tried hard enough, she could make a relationship happen. But she'd finally realized that she'd never been completely happy.

When the counselor tried to explain that she couldn't blame Beth for her depression, Stephanie had gotten angry and stormed out. She was even angrier at Beth after that, claiming she'd been ambushed in the session and refusing to see the counselor again. A few weeks later, she announced that she was seeing someone else and that she would be bringing her home. To their house.

In painful disbelief, Beth had finally blown up, telling

Stephanie that she would not allow that kind of shit. But it had happened anyway. She'd come home one day to find her lover with some woman from her office. Even though Beth's mind had raced with visions of gunshot wounds and hacked-up limbs, she'd shakily ordered them out of the house. After that, Stephanie moved into the guest room. Alone.

There was no official breakup, other than the one-time insertion of another woman into their home. The relationship was over and the woman never came back. Stephanie moved out.

In the months that followed, Beth had tried desperately to understand what had gone wrong, convinced that if she could just figure out what to do differently, Stephanie would come back. She didn't know why did she'd held on to such loyalty to Stephanie. She slapped a hand to her forehead, wincing because she'd used more force than intended.

"You wanted a relationship with someone who couldn't give it back. Get that through your brain," she said quietly as she rolled over onto her stomach, clutching the pillow in a tight embrace.

All she wanted was someone who wanted to be with her, someone who didn't pull the rug out from under her. She wanted an ordinary, secure relationship. In the meantime, she had to take care of herself. Maybe she shouldn't back away from Mary. What would it hurt to say yes to being with someone who made her laugh? That would be taking care of herself.

She would be seeing Mary tomorrow. The thought sent warmth coursing through her, starting in her toes and rising to her face. She sighed. She wanted to kiss her. She wanted Mary to hold on to her ass and pull her confidently in. But damn it, she still possessed the twisting feeling that she hadn't quite ended with Stephanie. Yet here she was fantasizing about Mary, who was amazing and sexy and captivating. How could something so wonderful to imagine feel like a betrayal of Stephanie? It was crazy.

Beth sat up. What did she owe Stephanie? *Move on, for shit sakes!* Mary was honest and exciting and breathtaking. And she was right here, wanting her. Also, by the way, stand Stephanie next to Mary, and who would any sensible woman step toward? Beth got off her bed and stared out the window toward the fading light of the sun, asking herself that question. The answer came instantly.

It sure as hell wouldn't be Stephanie.

Chapter Nine

Their walk was magnificent. The orange-vermilion color of the Golden Gate Bridge cut through the fog to the north, and all along the stretch of sand where San Franciscans walked their dogs, threw Frisbees, or sat on towels, writing and sketching in journals. The glorious panoramic view of the Pacific Ocean was breathtaking. The sun had been poking its head out of the low-lying clouds, shimmering behind an almost translucent fog that swirled in big, misty gray puffs.

Mary was glad she'd told Beth to bring something warm to wear. The crisp bay breezes cut through light clothing, and Beth had donned her sweatshirt right away. Mary drew in a deep breath of salty air and closed her eyes, tilting her face toward the sun. She came here as often as she could, but usually alone. She was contemplating removing her running shoes to feel the wet sand between her toes when Beth's hand slipped into hers.

"Thanks, Mary."

"For?"

"Bringing me here. This is better than a rest day."

Mary looked into the hazel eyes that constantly drew hers. Sometimes it seemed that they were different every time she studied them. At first, last week, they were glassy and remote, yet even then something had flickered from them. Mary was fascinated by those glimpses of the inner Beth and wanted to know more.

"Come with me," she said and Beth followed her away from the water to the sea wall.

They sat on the sand, their backs to the wall, and were sheltered somewhat from the breezes. The wall felt warm from the intermittent sun and they both hugged their knees up against their chests. They relaxed in silence, watching the beachgoers traverse the sand. Beth straightened one of her legs and reached down to massage her muscles. She angled her head toward Mary, pushing her light brown hair back. Her windblown cheeks glowed and her full, sweet mouth parted in a small smile that seemed private, as if she'd just thought of something that made her happy.

Mary wished she would share it but knew Beth was keeping her at a distance. Her reserve was always there, the legacy of a damaged heart. Every time they spoke, Mary could sense her suspicion and uncertainty. It came as no surprise. They were virtually strangers and Mary's reputation had no doubt preceded her. She could be certain that someone at the Coop had filled Beth in on her track record.

They thought she was a wild woman, living out loud and attracting women to her be-in-the-moment existence. The observations of various people gravitated back to her. Most believed she was open and unguarded about everything in her life, but that wasn't true. She gave herself fully to friendships and experiences and encounters, but there was one place where she allowed no one to venture. Her heart.

For years Mary had shielded that part of herself to most everyone. Keeping a furtive hold on her memories somehow preserved the love she'd needed so desperately to hold on to. But lately, she'd begun to realize that her precious secrets weighed like an albatross tied to her, keeping her locked in time. It was time to move forward. She could start by talking about what had happened.

She searched Beth's face, seeking the softness she was never able to disguise. Mary knew she tried, but her failure to keep up the facade of sophistication was part of her enchantment. Mary had always been a sucker for people who struggled to find their own strength, not simply expecting to be rescued. She saw that blend of willpower and vulnerability in Beth.

"Remember when you asked me if I'd ever had my heart broken?"

Beth's expression changed instantly. Her reflective tranquility was still present, but her eyes were more intent. "Yes."

"Well, I have." Mary drew in a deep breath. "Those lost years we were talking about at the party...I was living in West Hollywood. I was twenty-six. I loved the city. It was so openly gay and affirming. I worked at a grocery store, making enough money to pay the rent and little else, but it was such a free time. I was really happy."

Mary hesitated, trying not to feel guilty that she was about to open the door to a painful place she'd protected for so long. But this was for her, not for Gwen. "I was with a woman named Gwen. We were crazy in love and living in a studio apartment down the street from the Sunset Strip. I knew she was the one, you know?"

Beth nodded. The reserve had left her face entirely. Her gaze was tender and reassuring.

"We'd been together three years. One night, we had an argument." Mary laughed sadly. "I don't even remember what it was about. Gwen stormed off, saying she was going to the gym." Her throat tightened. She looked out over the sea, focusing on the horizon line. "She was crossing Santa Monica Boulevard. She had her workout bag in her hand. They said she was trying to beat a group of cars but something must have distracted her. Or she stumbled. No one seemed to see exactly how it happened."

"Oh, my God." Beth placed her hand on Mary's forearm, almost as though to signal that she didn't need to say any more, that Beth already knew what was coming.

But Mary had to let it out. She felt tears falling as she shaped the truth into words. "She was hit and thrown onto the windshield. She died before they reached the hospital."

The events unfolded again in her mind, as they had so many times before. There was no way to neutralize the facts. Exposing them briefly intensified the pain, then she was swamped with relief. She was grateful that Beth sat with her in silence. She needed time. The words had finally come out, cementing the reality she could not escape. But what had happened could now take its correct place in time rather than keeping her in a suspended state in her mind. It would always be a part of her, but she could exist beyond it. The secret had kept her stranded, with her heart locked away out of loyalty to Gwen. The only way to move on was to release its hold on her. And Beth, a woman she barely knew, had given her the impetus to do so.

Mary felt vulnerable and suddenly very tired. Examining the smaller hand still resting loosely on her arm, she said, "My heart broke into a million pieces that day." A weak smile formed through the pain that now could retreat, leaving her in a healthier place. "The lost years began shortly after that."

Beth pulled her into a hug, whispering, "I'm so sorry, Mary."

They held on to each other until they both started to shiver from the cold sand beneath them.

"Let me buy you a cup of coffee." Beth stood and offered her hand.

They'd parked close to the Java Beach Café and made their way up to the coffeehouse without speaking. Mary felt strangely light. She looked up as a shaft of bright sunlight fell across them. Overhead, an albatross soared. Smiling, Mary watched it vanish into the clouds.

"Ready?" Beth asked.

"Yes." Mary leaned over and kissed her cheek. "I think I am."

They spend the rest of the morning on lighter topics and got back to the Coop just before a downpour. Beth invited Mary in, but she shook her head.

"I need to get going."

Beth nodded. She, of all people, understood the need for time alone to deal with emotion. "Thank you for this morning…for everything."

She held the door, waiting for Mary to walk away. They looked into each other's eyes and Beth's pulse accelerated, but not just because of the pull of attraction she always felt. Mary wasn't looking at her as though she could see them naked together. She seemed to be offering something of herself, more than just her body, and inviting Beth to accept. Beth didn't know if anyone had ever looked at her that way.

"Would you like to go out tomorrow night?" Mary asked.

Beth's next breath jammed somewhere in her chest. "Is this a date?"

Mary's smile was slow but sure. "I would like it to be. Would you?"

Beth sifted through her instinctive trepidation, attempting to set aside the damage from her breakup. The lack of confidence. The urge to protect herself. *Allow yourself this*, she reasoned. But what did a date with Mary mean, exactly? Did it mean drunken debauchery? Did it mean sex? She'd enjoyed the innocent flirtation they'd engaged in. Up to now, she'd been able to be close to Mary without the complication of knowing her better.

Spending time with someone who didn't touch her emotions involved no risk, and a date would be the next natural step. Simple fun. Good for the ego. A stepping stone back to the woman she used to be. But Mary?

Beth acknowledged the curling apprehension in her gut. "I'm not sure."

"Let's not call it a date. We can just say we're booking some time together. How about a gathering of two?"

Beth's mind raced back and forth between the woman she was beginning to care for and relax around, and the woman of questionable repute. She hadn't felt imposed upon or played in the slightest, and their conversation on the beach had showed her a side of Mary she suspected few people saw. Still, that didn't mean Mary was a completely different person from the flirt Beth had seen at the party. Lord knew what she would do on a date. Calling it something else didn't change the simple fact that they each knew it wasn't just a walk, or a casual cup of coffee.

All the same, the new label conferred some breathing room, and Beth needed it. "Okay, a gathering of two, then. Tomorrow night."

"May I gather you at around seven?"

Beth laughed, relaxing a little more. "Yes, you may."

❖

"Pull up a rose," Alder said when Beth stepped out onto the back porch a few minutes later. She was trimming a bush full of yellow blooms. "Mary didn't stay long."

"She asked me out on a date."

"That's very nice."

"What the hell am I thinking? I can't go out with Mary." Beth blinked as if that would help clear some of the fog in her brain.

"Lighten up, Beth. It's just a date, not a wedding ceremony."

"It's a gathering…of two…" Beth trailed off.

Alder looked sideways from her flowers. "As long as you know what it is, you can call it anything you like. What the heck, it should be fun."

"Fun like a carnival or fun like grand theft auto?"

Alder laughed. "Who knows with Mary, but I certainly don't think you'll have a bad time."

"She's pretty bold, Alder. I don't know if I'm ready for that. I said I'd go, but I might live to regret it."

Alder snapped her head up, smiling into the sun. "Remember our pact? Regrets be damned."

"Regrets be damned," Beth repeated unconvincingly.

Alder snipped off a yellow rose and handed it to her. With a middle-aged heave-ho, she picked herself up and went inside. Beth followed her to the kitchen.

"What do you think she wants?"

Alder smiled. "What everyone wants."

"And what's that?" Beth asked, finding a vase for the rose.

"Good question. I recommend you answer it for yourself."

Beth faked a groan of dismay. "Are you always like this?"

"I try to be," Alder said, frustratingly Zen-like in her calm. She subjected Beth to a long look. "Were you on the beach today?"

Alder's intuition never ceased to amaze Beth. "How can you tell?"

"You have sand in your eyebrows." Alder cocked her head slightly and looked her up and down. "And you seem more…centered."

"You know something," Beth said, after considering the reply. "That's exactly how I feel."

CHAPTER TEN

At exactly seven o'clock Wednesday night, Mary was at the door of the Coop. Beth had washed her newest Levi's and a yellow button-down shirt. Not fancy, but clean and comfortable. Mary had on Levi's as well and a tight red short-sleeved shirt that hugged her curves.

"I didn't bring the car because I thought we'd stay in the Castro," she told Beth. "But if you wish, I live about eight blocks from here, so we could go get it."

"No," Beth said. "Castro's great." She liked the idea of a walking date. It seemed more casual, more innocent.

Possibly sensing Beth's anxiety, Mary kept the conversation light. When prodded, she shared a few Coop anecdotes, namely embarrassing ones about Dan's jaunty libido, Diane and Gina's constant roughhousing, and Alder's calming ways. She also told Beth about a false alarm, where a very drunk, very nude man had sat on a couch not long after spilling very spicy habañero sauce on the upholstery. He'd frantically called 911, screaming that he was on fire.

As they strolled toward Castro proper, Beth began to loosen up, but her caution was only slightly diminished.

"Feel hungry?" Mary asked, pausing to read a menu displayed on a restaurant window.

Beth nodded. "Famished."

They walked a little further until they came to a bistro where the clientele was not all twentysomethings and the music allowed conversation. Over drinks and appetizers, they exchanged stories about college, dream homes, and likes and dislikes. Mary was just as attentive toward Beth at dinner as she'd been at the party. But without the distraction of people pulling her in six directions, her concentration was more intense.

After the waiter delivered their entrées, she took Beth's hand, which quivered at the gentle but deliberate gesture. Beth disguised her reaction by squeezing Mary's hand firmly.

"That's the first law of thermodynamics," Mary said.

"The first…that all energy is constant?"

"Mmm-hmm." Mary grinned. "It remains constant. It cannot be created nor destroyed. After you talked about the second law, I got on the Internet."

"And what relevance does that have now?" Beth was not only curious about Mary's statement, she was delighted that Mary had remembered their talk and had even researched the topic.

"I feel my energy when I'm around you," Mary replied. "It moves from feeling excited when I see you to silly when we're joking. It's constant. And I feel the same with your energy. I felt it when I took your hand just now. And it makes sense that it may change form but it won't go away." She pulled Beth's hand to her lips and placed two delicate kisses on her knuckles.

"I have to admit you're right." Beth felt spellbound. "I feel an incredible amount of energy when I'm around you. Sometimes I don't know where to put it all."

"Just know that it will continue buzzing around us until

we either let ourselves go with it, or change the energy into something else."

That was why the urge to grab hold of Mary was so strong sometimes, while other times she gave in to the compulsion to run. Beth tried to relax, but her mind refused to relinquish its claim on the phrase "let ourselves go." She knew exactly where that energy would propel her, straight into the arms of a woman dangerous to her peace of mind. She slid her hand from Mary's grip and immediately lifted her iced water, using the drink as an excuse for her withdrawal.

They fell into an easy conversation about their childhoods and where they grew up. Beth cherished the feeling that Mary listened to every one of her words, absorbing what she said, asking relevant questions, and making her feel close to the center of the universe. Mary's focused intensity disarmed her. It had been much easier to be with her back at the party, in the middle of a lot of people and noise. Mary's attention had only been sporadic, but now it would span the whole evening as they finished their desserts then walked home. As much as she cherished being Mary's focal point, Beth also wanted to bolt. She was flattered, intellectually, to have such a beautiful creature concentrate on nothing but her, but her body squirmed.

Mary's beauty, her charm, and the obvious attraction people had for her all made Beth's head swim in a blend of fear and desire. She wanted to blame her state on the red wine, which was this side of velvety heaven, but she knew it was Mary who'd intoxicated her. And she was enjoying the heady feeling.

She wondered what the party would have been like had she not walked down from her room. Would Mary have chosen one of the women staring at her, that hot brunette perhaps?

Even if she hadn't, that night, she could at any future time. Women weren't going to stop hitting on her, regardless.

Beth concluded that, either way, it didn't matter. Whether Mary had many women or few bore no relevance to this current night. Beth wanted to go wherever the night took her, because all that mattered was the time they had right now. She couldn't predict anything and she refused to try; guessing at outcomes would only make her lose her nerve. She hoped she wouldn't live to regret this flirtation with recklessness.

When the waiter made his fifth pass by the table, coffeepot in hand, Beth realized it was a gesture of finality. They'd been there for three hours. Sheepishly, they paid the check, left a sizable tip for the lengthy stay, and headed back out onto the street. It was ten thirty and the Castro was alive at full throttle, the sidewalks streaming with pedestrians and the bars bursting at the seams.

Loud music rolled out onto the street and the throbbing bass beats rattled Beth's chest as they passed each drinking establishment. They were walking slowly, their hands clasped together.

"Tell me a dream, Beth."

"A dream? Like the ones you have at night or the ones you have in life?"

"Life. Those are better."

Beth nudged Mary teasingly. "Tell me one of yours, first."

"Fair enough. Let's see. I have a dream that one day I will be the first in the world to do something."

"What kind of something?"

"Oh, there are a couple of things. One is to be the first person to communicate with a being from another world…and have proof." She rolled her eyes impishly. "That probably sounds pretty corny."

"Not at all. It's interesting, actually."

Mary embellished on what must have been a well-thought-out image. "Can you imagine what you could talk about? I'd want to know where they were from and what their life was like. A million questions, for sure."

"Of course there would be the cover of *Time* magazine to deal with."

Mary turned her right cheek to Beth. "This is my best side, wouldn't you say?!"

Any side is your best side. Beth could definitely feel the wine. "What's another dream?"

"Hmm." Mary pondered, apparently trying to choose the right words. A flash of darkness crept across her face. The shadow that passed through her eyes was very nearly imperceptible in the artificial streetlights. "I guess I'd want to see people who've left, to have another moment with someone who's gone."

Beth immediately regretted asking Mary for her second dream. She'd invited her back to a painful place in her life, to those memories she'd obviously struggled with for a long time. She was about to apologize when Mary's eyes brightened.

"Okay, it's your turn."

Beth left her apology unspoken. What dreams had she had lately? She mulled the question over. There had been Stephanie's and her dream of living together forever. That had died a painful death. Any other dreams seemed to be submerged in a bowl of thick pea soup.

After Mary's revealing answers, her own seemed evasive. "Clarity, maybe."

"What kind of clarity?"

"Some clear, unclouded vision of what the heck my future will be. I don't know. Maybe to understand how to make a relationship work." Beth quickly added, "That must sound pretty lofty. I suppose a few million dollars falling from the sky would be a more likely possibility."

"Why?" Mary seemed genuinely puzzled.

"Achieving crystal clarity seems next to impossible. A dream like that is second in difficulty right behind discovering the meaning of life."

"No," Mary asserted. "That one's easy."

"The meaning of life?" Beth was more than intrigued. "Okay, I'm listening."

Mary stopped to face her. Grinning like a child with a secret, she wrapped her arms around Beth and lowered her face into Beth's neck. They hugged tightly and Beth felt Mary's breasts against hers. Instantly aroused, she drew in a mouthful of air and in the silence that followed, she could feel her heart pounding furiously. She was so dizzy, she was glad she could prop herself against Mary's body. Although that was also the problem. She wouldn't be hyperventilating if they weren't crushed firmly to each other, too close to talk.

Mary pulled back slightly. She smiled sleepily at Beth, then leaned in once more, and this time her lips lightly touched upon Beth's. They kissed, very softly. It felt as natural as breathing. Her lips moved tenderly over Beth's, caressing more gently than anyone had, in memory. And as naturally as it had started, the kiss ended.

For a moment, Beth stood there dazed. Mary took her hand, rubbing her palm gently, studying its lines and folds. When she smiled, Beth warmed inside. She liked the way Mary's concentration was absolute.

"I thought you were going to tell me the meaning of life." Her voice fractured slightly.

"I did," Mary said.

"Kissing?"

"It's living the simplest and truest of pleasures."

Mary hooked her arm into Beth's and they walked down the street, languid in their pace. In the silence that followed, Beth wondered if she could ever transcend to such a free and liberated place. Mary seemed to occupy her own sphere of certainty. Even with her sorrows and vulnerabilities, she seemed completely secure in herself. She knew who she was and didn't try to be someone else.

After inspecting a few bookstores and flower shops, they approached an adult store. Beth wasn't surprised when Mary pulled her inside to browse the aisles.

"Let's see what's new in fashionable sex." Mary grinned mischievously.

Doing what many fun-loving shoppers do, they giggled at the most outrageous sex toys and groaned at the biggest and longest. They made physical contact with each other quite a lot, grabbing an arm as they laughed, pushing a shoulder as they teased each other.

Mary picked up a dildo and waved it at Beth. "I don't miss these at all. The real ones, at least. Isn't it interesting, though, that while anatomically attached, these things are nothing but trouble, but when severed like this they can be a hell of a lot of fun. Don't you think?"

Beth marveled at Mary's gregariousness. She was bold in her feelings and thoughts and wasn't afraid to voice them. She wore her sexuality like a snug, sultry dress.

"What makes you think I'm not appalled by the thought of using a dildo?" Beth responded, feigning mild disgust.

Mary leaned toward her, using the fleshy instrument as a pointer. "You don't seem to be the kind of woman to shy away from a little fun."

Beth offered a noncommittal smile. "This is one of the few examples I can think of where it's men's turn to be reduced to an object. A piece of meat."

Mary raised the rubber member high in the air. "And this piece of meat comes with a free tube of lube. That's more than I can say for the real ones."

They laughed as Mary returned the dildo to its bin.

"I can tell you're not a stranger to these accessories," Mary said. "True?"

When Beth turned toward a rack of oils and lubricants, she felt Mary's hand on her shoulder. Her other arm slid around Beth's waist and she stood pressed against her back as they faced the display.

"You didn't answer my question," Mary whispered. Her breath was so warm on Beth's neck, she was afraid to turn around.

Swarming butterflies in her stomach kept Beth from answering. She felt herself flush, her legs and arms growing hot. This woman was definitely doing something to her, something very, very incredible. As Mary hugged her a little tighter, the feeling of those firm breasts pressed against her was undeniably provocative. Beth's breathing quickened, threatening to break into gasps. She wanted to reach out to steady herself but dared to lean back into Mary instead.

"I must admit," she was finally able to utter, "I've indulged in rubber fetishes before."

"Let me guess." Mary's voice lowered to a baritone hum. "They're not a sexual necessity, just an entertaining variation every once in a while."

Beth laughed. "You sound like a late-night radio psychologist. But, yes, I'd never replace a woman's touch or her tongue with a fake substitute. Still, now and then toys are amusing."

"I hear you. Never requirement, only recreation."

Beth stared straight ahead at the row of lubricants.

Several bore such alliterated names as "Midnight Moisture" and "Sultry Slick."

"That's a waste of money." Mary's whisper was as certain and resolute as a red-hot bullet, speeding through Beth's ear and slamming into her clit.

What was it about this woman? Did she know she was driving Beth out of the last remnants of her mind? They hardly knew each other and yet Beth felt she could pursue anything Mary suggested. Go anywhere Mary took her. *Stop me before I regret this.*

"How is it a waste of money?" she managed to say, feeling a dizzy sexual intoxication, wanting to hear more.

Mary turned her slowly around and looked into her eyes. "That kiss."

"Yes?" Beth croaked because suddenly she'd lost her voice.

She waited for more, but Mary's eyes just bored into her. The silence seemed unbearably drawn out. Beth remained locked into Mary's gaze, drinking in the goddess that stood before her.

Then Mary answered, this time sounding quietly vulnerable, "That kiss, Beth. It made me wet."

All the air escaped Beth's lungs, making her feel faint. Her head swirled. In that moment she understood this woman's power. Mary had a hard, strong body, but that wasn't it. She had a beautiful face that captured everyone's attention, but that wasn't it either.

Her power lay in the way she moved, the way she stood, the way she touched, the way she expressed her feelings, all rolled into one hot, fluid being. Either the sexual aura she possessed was a result of many intimate encounters, or those encounters were the result of a profoundly deep, natural-born current. Whichever scenario was accurate, all Beth could see in front of her was a fire she wanted to walk straight into. She hungered to be engulfed. It didn't matter that one could never walk into a fire and stay very long. Her throat was dry, which she found strange, when juxtaposed with the dampness she felt between her legs.

Oh, God. They were both wet.

Mary's eyes sparkled. "Suddenly, being in the company of all these sexual simulations isn't doing justice to you. Let's get out of here."

And though Beth was sure her legs wouldn't, couldn't move, she somehow managed to get back out onto the street. As naturally as before, Mary's hand found hers and they walked further through the Castro.

Beth inhaled the night air, getting oxygen back into her brain. She should admit that what had just happened was lunacy. She should. And while she was at it, she should remember that she was not the kind of person to walk into an impromptu moment and just spontaneously combust. But she made no admissions of the sort.

Instead she looked directly at Mary and said, "I'm wet, too."

Chapter Eleven

After a few blocks Mary pointed to a bar across the street. The patrons could be heard laughing and singing the full distance away.

"We've got to go inside." Mary grinned as they dodged traffic.

It was practically shoulder-to-shoulder people as they entered. The ratio of men to women was about equal. The vast majority had their proud gayness in common, but even the few who were more than likely straight were arm in arm with friends who most definitely weren't.

Beth immediately liked the feel of the place. No one in the jovial crowd seemed too drunk, nor was the music blaring so loudly that all anyone could do was stare at people or dance. The bar was actually a big rectangular island in the middle of the room, with bartenders holding court on every side. One of them held a microphone and was acting as emcee. Though there was music playing, he was definitely the main entertainment.

As they approached, a woman darted between them, moving in so close to Mary that they were almost nose to nose.

"Hey, baby." The woman's seductive smile was slightly exaggerated.

Mary stepped back and reached for Beth's hand. She seemed to know the woman. "Hey, how are you?"

"Beyond ready."

Mary ignored the innuendo. "Nice to see you," she said insincerely and continued leading Beth toward the bar.

More people greeted Mary, some waving as others reached out to hug her. When the emcee spotted her, he raised the mic and said, "Mary's here. Someone get her a drink, quick."

Other patrons yelled hellos and Mary just laughed.

The emcee raised a bottle of cinnamon schnapps over his head. He was very effeminate, which amused Beth because he seemed to be one of the strongest men there. His muscles bulged from inside his shirt and rippled down his forearms to the beefy paws that held the mic and the bottle.

He waved the schnapps. "Now all of you sports fans stay outta this one… I'm only talking to the men, now." Everyone howled, and he went on, "Oh, all right, lipstick lesbians included, too. First one to yell out the answer gets the schnapps. In nineteen seventy-one, which NFL team went totally undefeated through the season and on to win the Super Bowl?"

Mumbling broke out in the bar and a tall, thin man with a thick shock of red hair yelled out, "The Miami Dolphins."

The emcee feigned a heart attack and narrowed his eyes at the redhead. "Did you come up with that all by your lonesome, or did the softball team help you?"

There was, in fact, a group of women behind him, all sporting striped ball pants. One of the female players raised her hand and called out, "That was too easy. Ask a harder question."

"Oh well," the emcee waved a hand through the air, "I guess I underestimated the time you've sat in front of the telly watching locker-room interviews. Can't blame you, honey."

Suddenly from wherever the sound system was being controlled, a song came up, louder than before. Grand Funk's version of "The Locomotion" began and the emcee called out, "Yeah! Up on the bar!"

He was pointing to the women's softball team and, without hesitation, ten or twelve of the players jumped up onto the bar top and started lip-synching to the song at the top of their lungs. The rest of the patrons started clapping in time. It was obvious that these activities were a regular occurrence, which could explain why the bar was packed on a Wednesday night.

Beth and Mary sang and clapped along, glancing at each other and laughing. The emcee handed the mic to one of the softball players, and one by one they took solo choruses before passing it along. The song ended to a roar of applause and as soon as the next song started, the women jumped down and various men leapt up to take their place. They all started singing and more and more of them climbed up until the bar top was packed. The bartenders stopped serving drinks and stood back to watch.

The emcee had the mic again and the music faded into the background. He made a grand gesture of looking at his watch and yelled, "Do you know what time it is?"

In boisterous unison, the crowd yelled, "It's Chubby Bunny Time."

Beth looked to Mary. "What?"

"You'll see," was Mary's answer as she put her arm around her.

From behind the bar the emcee pulled out a huge stainless steel bowl filled to the brim with large, plump white marshmallows. He called out, "Raise your hand if this is your first time here."

As most of the crowd chuckled, about ten or fifteen people held up their hands. Beth remained motionless, but felt her hand being raised by Mary. Before she could muscle it back down, the emcee spied them.

"Mary. You've brought a virgin. I'm gonna have to tell your ex about this. That is, if I could narrow it down to a few...hundred."

The crowd cheered as Mary shot him a dirty, but smiling, look.

"I'm just jealous 'cause you're so gorgeous. What's her name?"

"Beth," Mary called.

"Well, Beth, come on up here."

Beth's hesitation lasted only as long as it took Mary to gently push her toward the emcee. Beth took his hand and stepped up onto the bar. As another "virgin" was hauled up, Beth looked out over the cheering crowd and wondered what in the name of Moses had gotten her to this bar top. She was very aware of two distinct personalities dueling inside her, one that would have normally been home enjoying a quiet evening, and a new alien woman with seemingly no command of restraint.

Beth looked down at Mary. Her face glowed in the light of the bar and she winked the sexiest, most wonderful wink that had ever been directed at Beth. Her knees felt like rubber. She couldn't concentrate on the instructions from the emcee about the bar game underway.

He held the bowl of marshmallows in front of her and said, "No chewing, no swallowing," then called, "Hey, Mary? Does Beth swallow?"

Cool as a cucumber, Mary replied, "She's too much of a lady to tell."

Look at her up there, she thought. Beth was beautiful. Mary couldn't remember the last time she'd wanted to get to know someone so deeply. Usually after a couple of dates or a quick sexual encounter, Mary's interest abruptly waned. It wasn't that she was hard to please. It was that she never felt a significant connection, in part because she hadn't allowed it to happen. That was her fault. Still, she continued to meet women and go out on dates. Some led to bed. Some didn't. But all of them led to the realization that there weren't any sparks.

Beth was the exception. Since they first met, Mary's interest had only increased. Beth was fascinating and clever and sexy as hell. She was a million miles ahead of every other woman Mary had been around since Gwen. Her heart thrummed faster as she watched Beth up on the bar. She knew Beth was still feeling stung by her last relationship; it was evident from her skittishness. Mary's efforts to gain her trust seemed to be working, but she was cautious.

It would have been too easy to hurry Beth back to her place, or to the Coop, after their conversation at the sex toy store. Yet she wasn't willing to back off and deny herself these new and scary feelings. She felt more alive in her heart than she'd been in years. Fear and joy careened around her brain like two cats chasing one fly.

She watched Beth cramming marshmallows into her mouth and trying to repeat the "chubby bunny" catch phrase as the crowd clapped and whistled. An explosion of cheers drowned out the emcee as he finally announced her the winner. Beth was too busy spitting out the marshmallow mess to accept a bottle of peppermint schnapps, so Mary stepped up, laughing uproariously as she took it.

"You're my hero," she teased as she helped Beth down and wrapped her arms around her. As the kudos and pats on the back subsided, she said, "I'd love to continue our walk through Castro, if you'd like."

Beth nodded. "I'd like that."

They gave the schnapps to the emcee's other victim and

slipped out of the bar. Out on the street, Mary threw an arm around Beth.

"How are you doing, chubby bunny?"

"I thought I was your hero." She feigned hurt but was still laughing too much to be convincing.

Mary stopped her and they stood, face-to-face, in front of a nearby restaurant. Beth glanced at the two tables closest to the restaurant window. One was occupied by a gay male couple, the other by a straight couple.

"You *are* my hero." Mary smiled mischievously. Her eyes danced in the soft light spilling from the restaurant's small awning. "Later, I want you to show me again how you ate all those marshmallows."

"I didn't eat them," Beth said softly. "I took them into my mouth and held them…with my tongue."

She realized that what she'd just said was the kind of bold comment Mary might have made. But somehow, being with such a sexy, uninhibited woman made Beth feel she could say anything that came to mind. And she was sloshed, not to mention aroused. She knew she should pull the reins back a bit. Fun was fun, but Mary was not the kind of woman who made for a reliable lover.

Beth reasoned with herself yet again that she was planning to enjoy tonight, no matter what. She wasn't spending time with Mary because she saw a future for them. She had no romantic illusions. Glancing around, she felt slightly self-conscious. The restaurant couples were gazing at them. The gay pair just smiled, but the straight couple stared more intently. Here, right in front of them, were two lesbians engaged in some kind of foreplay. Beth couldn't tell if she saw curiosity or condemnation on their faces. Gay-bashing was always a threat, but it seemed highly unlikely that this couple would produce baseball bats and chase them down the street, especially in the Castro. If they didn't want to see gays or lesbians showing affection in public, why eat in this neighborhood? Maybe they were not quite as hip as they thought.

"They seem more interested in us than their Crab Louie, don't they?" Mary said, also observing the uncomfortable-looking couple.

And with a defiance that was undoubtedly second nature to her, she planted a wet kiss on Beth's lips. It was quick and delicious, and before Beth could react, Mary was nuzzling her neck, sending tantalizing bolts up her spine. The straight couple looked away, the woman fidgeting and the man frowning.

If this had happened anywhere else, with anyone else, Beth knew she would have been irritated at being made part of the show. But she was keenly aware that there was something special about Mary that not only made her impulsive behavior okay, but exciting and adventurous.

Maybe Mary had placed her under some sort of mysterious spell. Beth already welcomed the thought of mild sexual possession, possibly more. There was no doubt that being here with Mary felt wonderfully irresponsible and stimulating. Certainly anyone could speculate that Mary had some special powers. Powers of enticement and charisma. But Beth suspected part of her appeal was the fact that she lived with such freedom and in-your-face honesty. Her seeming lack of concern with her image entranced Beth. She felt like a devoted student, losing herself in the exhilaration of Mary's teachings.

Still, she knew she could never be with a woman so unbridled. At least, not for anything serious. Mary was not the kind of woman she would want in her life long-term. She needed a woman who was stable and reserved and predictable. That was the best relationship material.

Right now she was on a wild roller-coaster ride and

was not yet ready to get off. She absolutely, positively, did not know where the ride was going to take her—but it didn't matter. Normally her lack of concern would have worried her. But she was having too much fun and she wanted some new, happy memories to take back home with her.

Regrets be damned.

The air grew damp as they walked hand in hand around the Castro. They shared more stories as they strolled up and down the dark, Victorian-lined streets. Beth wasn't exactly sure where she was. They were probably not far from the Coop or Castro Street, but all she cared about was that she was a million miles from L.A.

"Come here," Mary whispered, taking Beth's wrist and pulling her between the narrow squeeze of two Victorian houses.

Beth's pulse raced as she laughed nervously. "What's with you and the 'come here' thing?"

"I like getting you alone," Mary growled, maneuvering between crates, hoses, and recycling bins as she tugged Beth as far back as possible between the two tall houses.

An alarm went off in Beth's head. Mary was trouble and she was letting herself be led right into it. What was the matter with her? But in a crazy way, she wanted to follow. She had to see where this would take her.

Mary backed up to the side of one of the buildings, drawing Beth close. "Plus," she said, "you're driving me crazy."

At once, her breasts were against Beth's. They kissed, arms tightly around each other, body to body. Beth shifted her leg for balance and crashed against a full-to-the-brim recycling bin. The sharp clinking of bottles made them freeze. And as they did, a light flashed on from a window above. Beth held her breath, waiting to see what the homeowner would do, but Mary engulfed her mouth again, erasing any concern about their trespassing. From a second-story window in the building right behind, two men laughed loudly, oblivious to the foreplay occurring just below them.

Just as one of the men yelled, "You're such a lovable bitch, Kenneth," their stereo drowned out their voices and the Rolling Stones' "Sympathy for the Devil" blared from the window. Somewhere in the back of Beth's mind, racing between Mary's breasts and her salty throat, came a fleeting thought that that particular song, playing at this particular moment, probably wasn't just mere coincidence.

As Mary's hands roamed the length of Beth's ribs before pausing at the rise of her breasts, Beth lifted her arms a little to make room for the warm caresses. Mary sucked gently on her neck, her fingers dancing close to Beth's nipples. Something deep and instinctive took over as Beth ground her hips into Mary and lifted her chin, offering more of her neck.

I can't help myself, she said to herself, hoping the excuse was good enough to silence the little voice that kept urging her to stop. As Mary's fingers found the tautness of her nipples, Beth shuddered, sucking in a breath. "Mary…" Her voice emerged as a deep and raspy murmur.

Mary paused. "I love your moan."

She licked the length of Beth's neck, down to her collarbone and back up to the underneath of her chin. Beth arched further, driven into hot arousal by the licks and nips and kisses. She found Mary's hands and cupped them to her breasts, moaning more loudly as Mary gently pulled at her very taut, very attentive nipples.

"Kiss me," Beth demanded through a wide, satisfied smile.

Mary's mouth met hers and her hands moved down to the band of Beth's Levi's. "You have just the right curves," she breathed between kisses.

One hand followed the seam of Beth's jeans, working up and down, closer and closer to the damp join between her thighs. Beth growled into Mary's throat and lifted her hips, craving more pressure where she was wet and swollen. Mary lightly massaged her through her Levi's, brushing across her crushed flesh with increasing urgency.

Beth was spinning quickly away to a place she knew Mary was more than willing to take her. She'd just met this woman a few days before and now they were between two strange houses, five hundred miles from Beth's home, and in some bizarre way it all seemed to make perfect sense. A strange, eccentric, desire-driven lucidity prevailed where Beth had once had doubts and fears. Nothing else needed to exist.

She traced a finger over one of Mary's hard, fabric-covered nipples, eliciting a deep moan. She relished the sensation of her pants seam pushing against her extremely full lips and rocked under Mary's light, grazing touch. Mary tugged at the top button of Beth's 501s. The buttonholes slid easily away from the buttons.

"Yes," Beth sighed. She wanted Mary to touch her, to feel her wetness.

Mary eased her hand into the tight, warm space between Beth's legs and groaned at what she found. "You are pure, silky heaven."

Beth bit into Mary's neck as she felt her pubic bone cupped. Mary slowly massaged Beth's mound of hair, her fingers working their way further between her legs. Beth could feel herself swelling. She turned her face toward Mary to catch her mouth. They kissed deeply, their moaning camouflaged by the Rolling Stones, whose haunting, pounding riffs swirled like alcohol in Beth's brain.

She reached around to cup Mary's ass with both hands, practically lifting her off the ground. Mary's silky, wet fingers still hadn't moved inside, and Beth knew why she was holding back. Mary, just like her, was luxuriating in the heat of this intoxicating moment. Beth savored the control Mary had imposed, and the sheer rush of anticipation it caused.

Firm admonishments scratched at the back of her brain. *Don't do this. Don't get into this type of trouble. This is not you!* But the thought of guiding Mary's fingers inside her, knowing she'd be steamy hot and wetter then she could ever have imagined, sent bolts of lightning smashing through her brain. From the first time she'd ever experienced this heady arousal, she'd craved the feeling like no other. Nothing equaled the high right before she touched a woman or a woman touched her. It felt like a drug. A drug of such supreme power, she could not resist its affects. Mary's all-consuming control only made Beth crave more.

She was soaked. Mary matched her gyrations and then, as Beth's heart pounded in her chest, she felt Mary's fingers curl up, tentatively parting her.

"I want you inside me," Beth rattled out, urging more. Her voice was low and scratchy. She felt raw.

Mary eased one, then two fingers inside. Beth closed her eyes as her head spun backward. She heard Mary growl from the bottom of her throat as she slid slowly in and out.

Beth moaned loudly. "Deeper, Mary. Deeper." And when Mary obliged, she gasped out a fierce, "Yeah."

Mary plunged her fingers upward, propping Beth more firmly against the wall, as though sensing that her legs were fast approaching collapse.

"We need a bed," Beth panted.

"No, we don't."

"If I come this way," Beth gulped between words, "you're going to have to carry me back to the Coop."

Mary looked into her eyes, smiling. "I live closer."

Beth was desperate. "Where?"

"Ten thirty-three Temple Avenue. But we're not going there."

"Please…"

"No, I want you. Right here."

And they kissed again, Mary moving deeper inside. Beth got wetter. She'd never had sex in an alleyway. And as far as she could remember, she'd never come standing up. She gripped Mary, squeezing her closer until they both began to tremble. Beth's legs shook wildly and she stammered one last plea. "Lay me down. Anywhere."

Mary whispered, "No."

The excitement of being taken that way sent Beth sailing over the edge. She shuddered and felt Mary's fingers gripped in her contractions. Her loud moans almost drowned out the Stones as she came once, then again, gushing over Mary's hand in strong, muscular pulses.

Minutes later, she was still panting, unable to speak.

"I just might have to carry you home," Mary said.

A wooden housing of electrical meters sat against the wall about two feet away, and Mary helped Beth over, lifting her up to sit on the three-foot-high box. Beth leaned over her, resting on her shoulder. Mary held her close until Beth's breathing slowly started to regulate.

Beth kissed her, groaning, "I can't feel my legs."

"Just stay right here with me." Mary held her even tighter.

Another light went on inside the building behind them. Voices of a man and woman filtered down from a high window. Beth hoped they weren't calling the cops, or worse, observing them through binoculars.

Mary lifted her down and helped her stand. She began buttoning up Beth's jeans. "I think we've pushed our luck long enough. Alder will kill me if she has to come bail us out of jail for copulating against someone's wall."

Beth raised an eyebrow. Her blood still raced from her orgasm and all she could think about was crawling deep inside Mary. She ached to touch her. "You're not serious."

Mary grinned. "Yes, I am."

Beth's voiced cracked. "You know this makes me want you even more."

Mary leaned toward her and whispered, "I hope so."

CHAPTER TWELVE

For a moment, Beth didn't know where she was. Bright light pounded through her eyelids. In the grog that was her mind, she reasoned it must be morning. With her eyes clenched shut, she listened for anything that sounded familiar. Nothing registered, so she braved a quick look at her surroundings.

She was alone in her room at the Coop.

"Shit," was all she could mumble.

Distracted from lack of sleep, she labored to remember how she'd ended up here when she was supposed to be in Mary's bed. Things the night before had gotten confusing. The encounter in the alley had been incredible, but on their way to Mary's place Beth's head began to fill with confusion. She'd opened up to Mary in ways she hadn't expected. Caught up in the moment, she'd wanted to make love to Mary and send her over the edge just as Mary had sent her. With the force of her own orgasm screaming in her brain, she'd felt half complete. All she could think about was seducing the woman responsible for her unbelievable *petite mort*.

A tangle of thoughts pinballed around in her brain. What was she doing? She'd only known Mary for five days. This was not where Beth's life was supposed to go. She didn't have spontaneous sex with women in dark alleys. She had stable relationships with stable women. As much as she desperately wanted to return the pleasures Mary had given her, she also felt alarmed. Her attraction to Mary had led her to make decisions that were out of character.

If she hadn't met Mary, she wouldn't have been in that alley. Beth had decided to experience whatever the night brought, but having sex in a public place wasn't what she'd had in mind. What disturbed her most was that she'd loved every minute. Apparently, since meeting Mary, she'd undergone a drastic personality change.

Beth sighed. No such thing had happened, of course. She was still the Beth Standish whose relationship had failed and whose partner found her boring. To escape the pain of that reality, she'd allowed a deeply buried part of herself to take over for a while. In hindsight, she could see her behavior in context. She'd wanted to be a different Beth for a while, unaffected by the hurt, happy and free and desired by a sexy woman like Mary.

But even as they'd started walking to Mary's place, Beth knew she wasn't being completely honest with herself. It would be okay if she could just take a time-out to enjoy herself with a gorgeous woman then return to her life. But it wasn't that simple and she knew if she spent the rest of the night with Mary, leaving would get even more complicated. The night that had been going so fantastically well got all jumbled in her brain at that point, and she wanted to bolt. From the alley, the evening, and Mary. As panic set in, she collected herself enough to ask Mary to walk her home, feigning tiredness. Whether or not Mary had believed the ruse, she had politely obliged, leaving Beth on the stoop with a fiery smile and a soft kiss on the lips.

Lying in her bed now, Beth felt despondent and confused.

She didn't know if she'd made the right choice for the right reasons, or if she'd been crazy. Her head ached and a keen throbbing behind her eyes drove her from under the covers and over to the bathroom sink.

She gasped as she splashed ice cold water on her face. Staring at her pale cheeks in the mirror, she said, "What the hell was I thinking?"

❖

Beth spent Thursday afternoon in Chinatown, shopping and eating. Since it was also a rest day from running, when she got back to the Coop, she read for a couple of hours and then enjoyed a long, hot shower. She changed into her black Levi's and pulled on a faded T-shirt she'd earned running a 10K race in Huntington Beach a few years back. It was well worn and the fabric was thin. Comfort clothing.

The whole bottom floor of the Coop was quiet except for the hum from the steadfast refrigerator. The living room was fairly dark; only a single lamp glowed in the corner. Beth sat down on the couch and laid her head back. The cars that passed by the window droned in a rhythmic cadence that felt comforting.

With her eyes closed, she could deduce the makes of various cars she heard. The *plat, plat, plat* of a Volkswagen was easy to recognize. The mechanical hum of a few Volvos was distinctive. And a Mercedes, like her own, was as easy to discern as the city bus, whose brakes squealed and hissed as it slowed to turn the nearby corner.

Beth took a deep breath and tried to relax. She could hear a few women walking down the street. They were laughing and talking in loud, energetic voices. Wherever they were going, whatever they were planning to do, it sounded like fun was to be the only option. Mary bounded gracefully into her thoughts, refusing to be ignored for more than a few minutes. Beth stared at the ceiling. An intoxicating warmth flowed through her as she recalled Mary's touch. Her scent. Her lips. She'd had sex in an alley. Standing up. It had been utterly impulsive and totally irrational. Completely unlike her. And it had excited the hell out of her.

Who was this woman who'd calmly invaded her life, stating very blatantly that she was attracted to her? With more confidence than anyone deserved to have, Mary had not only hit on her in a bathroom at the party, but pulled her between those houses for sex. Beth couldn't imagine being so impulsive from the get-go. If she were to draw a picture of Mary, it would be of a sexy, beautiful woman stepping off a cliff and smiling a huge, wide smile. Everyone watching would be gasping at such a daring exploit, only to then become envious of her spirit because not only did she enjoy the trip down, she also laughed aloud as she landed, unharmed, in an immense mound of feathers.

Beth had felt a similar exhilaration with Mary in the alley, and she normally didn't let things like that happen to her. Sure, she could be as fun as the next person, but only after getting to know her lovers and trusting them. Though in the recesses of her brain, she knew what she was doing was reckless, it had excited her to the core. She'd come harder than she'd ever remembered.

Beth shifted on the couch, aroused. The memory of Mary's fingers buried inside her caused a tightness in her chest that puzzled her. She didn't know if she felt lust, longing, anxiety, or excitement. She was beginning to understand the sweetness of that freedom and exhilaration Mary lived her life savoring. It was fantastic, but scary. What precarious door had she opened? A sobering notion seized her: being given a peek at a treasure was worse than never seeing it.

Beth shook her head. She could never be as impulsive as Mary. She was a responsible individual. But being brought to a shattering orgasm, in the dark space between two anonymous buildings, while being serenaded with "Sympathy for the Devil," was not exactly normal. Then again, nothing in her life was normal of late.

Too keyed up to remain on the couch, she got up and grabbed her car keys. As she slipped downstairs she checked her watch. Ringing the doorbell at eight at night wasn't exactly proper, but she was sick of torturing herself. Who was she kidding, anyway? She wasn't sorry that she'd had sex with Mary; she was only sorry she couldn't cope with casual encounters the way most people did. Perhaps she needed a little more practice.

She parked outside Mary's apartment and strolled to the door as though she wasn't nervous at all. And what, by the way, was she doing there? Hell, she knew damn well what she was doing there. Mary was Mary, and since Beth couldn't stop thinking about her, why not see her in person?

She listened for noises through the door. Less from a desire to carry out her spontaneous plan and more from a need to get off the landing in case someone mistook her for a stalker, she rang the bell.

Mary's face immediately brightened when she saw Beth. She grabbed her sleeve and pulled her inside saying, "I'm so glad you came by."

"Am I interrupting?"

"No, not at all. I was just getting ready to go out, but I think I've changed my mind." She paused, her eyes glistening in the low light of her apartment. "You remembered my address."

"I remember everything you said last night."

Mary stepped closer. "I'm flattered. Come on in."

She led Beth into a comfortable room with a bay window that looked out over the street. A plush, dark green couch blended well with a solid wood coffee table and several bookcases. Virtually every piece of artwork that hung on the walls was a signed and numbered lithograph, all by notable artists. Beth took in an eight-by-ten photograph of a woman wrapped up in a parka. She was exiting a cabin. Her broad smile, through a light snowfall, radiated intimate warmth. Beth knew immediately that she was looking at Gwen, the lover Mary had lost in the car accident. There were no other pictures of women. Beth surmised she hadn't had anyone in her life since Gwen. Looking for Ms. Right did not seem to be high on Mary's list.

Beth watched her walk over to the couch and couldn't help but drink in Mary's long legs. She had on comfortable shorts and a tank top. A tremble shuddered inside her as she remembered how those legs felt pushed up against her in the alley. She cradled her trembling hands in her lap. She felt the need to explain her visit but couldn't conjure up a solid reason. She didn't want to go out to dinner, didn't want to drag Mary out to the latest epic flick. She just wanted to see her.

"I really didn't have any reason to come by."

"Other than you wanted to?"

Beth watched Mary's full, sexy lips form each word. "Yes. Well, I did have a reason, actually. I wanted to apologize for ending the evening so…abruptly." *And I want to tear your clothes off.*

Mary smiled warmly. It was as if she could see everything that was flying around in Beth's head. "Last night was wonderful. No need to apologize."

"You're not mad that you went home by yourself?"

"You had your reasons. And I had a great time with you."

"I'm sorting some things out in my head." Beth paused. "But getting to know you has been really nice."

Mary nodded. "No worries."

She lowered her gaze to Beth's thighs, lean and shapely in her black jeans. *I'd like to know more about you,* she thought, curious about Beth's agenda. It was hard to guess from her face what she was thinking and feeling. Her hands gave her away. She couldn't keep them still.

Mary felt an odd awakening inside. She wanted to take those hands and kiss each of them, but she could sense a tightly coiled energy in Beth and didn't want to scare her into another rapid retreat. She'd almost gone over to the Coop earlier, which would have been a thousand times better than going to a bar, but something had stopped her. Such a reserved action on her part should have baffled her, but she knew it was because Beth was not like most women she met.

As they'd spent time over the past week running and talking, a reverence about their friendship had grown. She wasn't sure what effect last night's encounter would have on their budding connection, so she was relieved that Beth had come by. Hopefully they could clear the air. She'd been about to set out for the Lexington to unwind over a beer, but didn't suggest the idea to Beth, preferring to have the time alone with her.

"Are you going back to work tomorrow?" Beth asked.

"No, I've taken the rest of the week off to train."

"I can imagine firefighting is pretty dangerous."

"It can be," Mary said but realized that, right now, firefighting wasn't nearly as dangerous as the feelings she was having for Beth. "Mostly, it's hours of sheer boredom punctuated by moments of absolute exhilaration."

Beth laughed. "You must get a lot of dates while wearing that uniform." She immediately regretted the remark. She knew what the answer would be and cringed, not really wanting to talk about Mary's bountiful conquests.

Mary shrugged. "Mostly, we're sweaty and smoky and all I can think about is getting back to the station for a shower. But one fun thing about the whole firefighting thing was the film crew that followed us around for a week last summer."

"What were they shooting?"

"Some footage for an action movie. They wouldn't tell us who was in it."

"Did they get what they were looking for?"

"Raging fires, you mean? Yeah, there was a hell of a warehouse blazer. We shot out of the firehouse so quickly we nearly lost them. Then when they finally got to the warehouse, there were five battalions fighting the fire and they had trouble maneuvering around all the hoses and firemen and trucks. The chief finally let them stand on the top of our truck to shoot."

"So one day I might see you in the background of the next Tom Cruise movie?"

"Hopefully it'll be in the background of an Angelina Jolie movie." Mary grinned.

"So, you have a weakness for a Hollywood babe?"

"You caught me. I rather enjoyed the fight scene she had with Brad Pitt in *Mr. and Mrs. Smith*."

Beth laughed. "So did I."

"As a matter of fact, when the movie first came out, I liked the opening location so much that I bought a ticket and flew to Bogota for a vacation."

"You did? Was your visit as exciting as Angelina's?"

"No."

"You mean you didn't get your man?" Beth asked innocently. Damn, she had to stop talking about sex.

"I guess I got the woman." Mary paused. "You'll probably find it a bit crazy…"

Probably. But for some dimwitted reason, Beth wanted to know. "Try me."

"Well, there was a little gay bar not far from my hotel. I met this woman. I explained to her what had motivated me to fly down there. The next thing I knew, she'd taken me back to her hotel room."

"And you were wrestling around just like Brad and Angelina."

Mary's sheepish nod was as humble as it was comical.

Beth was not exactly surprised by the story. "You're not much for premeditation."

"No. The more I overthink something, the less fun it is when I finally do it. Usually."

Beth glanced down at Mary's neck. It looked absolutely edible. *I want you.* "Does that go for everything?"

"No." Mary looked thoughtful. "I thought about you a lot after I first met you, and that was fun. I was talking about chance moments. Serendipitous opportunities. You either stop to think about the consequences or you just react. I don't believe in letting anything slip by."

Mary's face radiated her convictions. Beth envied her. "That's a very freeing belief. I guess I should be thankful, since it got me between those two Victorians with you."

Mary laughed. "You're secret's safe with the three of us ladies."

"I don't think I consider it a secret."

"I thought that maybe, because of how the night ended, that you might have wanted it that way."

"No. At least I don't think so." *What I want is to take you to bed.*

"Sounds like you're not used to spontaneity, Beth."

"Not excessively." Beth wanted to examine her feelings more closely, but she was already chickening out and thinking about leaving.

"Oh, come on. You mean to tell me you've never been impulsive?" Mary teased. "You've never jumped off an ocean pier just because you saw was a dolphin out there? Or run after the ice-cream truck as soon as you heard the music?"

"Things like that? Of course I have."

"Then what's all the brouhaha?"

"Those things are different," Mary said. "I'm not as impulsive as you."

"What's the difference between running after ice-cream trucks and getting pulled into alleys?"

"One led to sex." The reply was abrupt but to the point.

Mary didn't try concealing her smile. "Regrets?"

A rigid chortle burst from Beth. "No." She cleared her throat. "It's just…sex doesn't usually happen that way for me. Don't get me wrong, it was great with you. I'm just surprised at myself."

Mary leaned forward until their noses touched gently. They were so close, Beth could feel Mary's breath on her face, warm and sweet. Mary kissed her lips gently and then pulled away. Beth's head spun and she tried fruitlessly to send a steadying message to her shaky legs.

Mary whispered, "Did you want to kiss me as much as I wanted to kiss you just then?"

Beth managed to whisper back, "Yes."

"Well, there's only one difference between you and me, really." Mary's eyes blazed into Beth's.

"What is that?"

Mary kissed her again. "You *think* it, and I *do* it."

Chapter Thirteen

I was getting ready to ground you," Alder said when Beth returned to the Coop. She was relaxing on the couch, leafing through a thick hardback novel.

Beth laughed and plopped down on the carpet in front of Alder. "It's only ten thirty, and you said I could stay out on a school night if I got my homework done."

"And did you?"

"Not really. I spent the entire afternoon doing nothing more than sitting and thinking."

Alder nodded. "Amazing how far such simple measures can get you."

Beth thought about her trip to Mary's place. They'd talked for over two hours. And Mary was right; Beth did think about things while others did them. Even as Mary had said that, Beth had wanted to push her down on the couch and rip her shirt off. But all she ended up doing was leaving.

"Alder, do you ever just say to hell with it and do something crazy?"

"Like when you packed your bag and just drove the hell out of L.A.?"

"Yes, like that. But have you ever been even crazier?"

"I imagine I've had my share of impulsiveness."

"Doesn't it seem…a little socially unacceptable?"

"Why should you worry what others think?"

"Because we live in a society where we're judged by their opinions."

"Hogwash." While Beth was absorbing that rather heavy stream of consciousness, Alder expounded on her theme. "Sometimes we spend so much time worrying about what others want that we forget to ask ourselves what *we* want. And then *you* just go do it, and pay no penance for it."

Beth smiled. "Regrets be damned?"

Alder high-fived her, repeating, "Regrets be damned!"

Beth got up and stretched. "Thanks for the talk…again."

"Thank you. I love having my brain exercised."

Beth got up.

"Where are you going, young lady?" Alder asked.

"To do what I want to do."

She headed for the front door, but not before hearing Alder's endearing boom of a laugh. "Good girl. Just don't get arrested."

Beth heard Mary yell, "Just a minute," and then the door was unlocked.

Glancing at her watch, Beth realized it was just before eleven. She sucked in a breath as the door opened. Mary wore nothing but a large white bath towel. Her cleavage peeked out over the top as she clutched the fabric to her.

"Hello again," she said.

They stood facing each other in the entryway. Beth wished she'd given a little more thought to what she was going to say.

"I wasn't ready to leave before."

"Well, that's good." Mary smiled. "Because I was starting to take it personally."

"You were?"

"No." Mary reached for her, pulling her inside.

Her warm palm melted softly into Beth's wrist. She reached around to close the door, causing the towel to loosen slightly over her full breasts. They stood facing each other, perilously close.

Beth had second thoughts. "It's late. Maybe this isn't—"

"I was just getting into the shower," Mary said, smoothly sweeping Beth's sudden anxiety aside. "Care to wait? I'll be right out."

Beth nodded mutely, searching for the words that would tell Mary what she wanted. Before she could think of any, Mary was sauntering down the hall.

"Make yourself at home," she called. "I won't be long."

Mary ran shampoo through her hair and rinsed as quickly as she could. Since Gwen, she hadn't felt the need for anything more than uncomplicated pleasures and simple distractions. She was always good to the women she spent time with, but she could never relax into them and feel deep passion. It was safer to keep the encounters light, even during sex. She'd once been called a butterfly by a woman she'd seen for a few weeks, and it hadn't been a compliment. Butterflies, the woman had told her, alight without much obligation and just fly away at the lightest disturbance.

Truth be known, she was right. Not since Gwen had Mary even entertained the idea anything serious; she just wouldn't let her heart go there. But from the moment she'd seen Beth sitting on the Coop's back porch, she was transformed somehow. It was like she'd awoken from a long, dark dream full of unfulfilled cravings and loneliness. Later, when she spent time with Beth at the party, she knew in her heart that she was a distinctly exceptional woman. She was excited that Beth had returned and aware of the significance of that decision.

No one could replace what she'd had with Gwen, but for the first time in years, Mary felt hopeful. The change made her exultant, as did the sensations of deep desire. But could she let herself go with those feelings?

Beth's wobbly legs found the big green couch again and she sat on the edge, her elbows resting on her knees. She fought off an urge to escape while Mary was in the shower. She felt jumpy. *What are you doing here, Beth Standish?*

Only an hour ago, she'd left after rambling on about this and that, wanting Mary more than she could ever admit. Then she'd made this big statement to Alder and headed straight back here. She looked down the hall toward Mary's room and listened to the soft spurting of the shower. What she pictured on the other side of the bathroom door make her light-headed. Was she crazy?

"Yes, I am," she said, rising to walk down the hall.

Visions of what Mary had done to her between the Victorian houses deluged her brain. Mary had literally taken her. It was hot and spontaneous but only half complete. She passed Mary's down comforter–covered bed, heading for the bathroom. The door was slightly ajar, steam rolling out like fog off the coast. She inhaled the scents of shampoo and soap. The glass door to Mary's shower was tinted slightly, with a grouping of shells etched into the glass. Hands over her head, breasts full and swelling, Mary was rinsing her hair. When she opened her eyes, a smile blazed brightly across her face.

Without any words, Beth stepped in and her mouth quickly found Mary's. The kiss was fervent and impassioned, punctuated by moans. Hot water poured over them, soaking Beth's clothes. Mary's body was slick with soap, every smooth muscle inviting Beth's touch. She pushed against her as determinedly as Mary pushed back. Their tongues danced as Beth quickly found Mary's breasts, squeezing softly. She lowered her mouth to suck one nipple with just enough pressure to induce excited cries from Mary.

Her hands landed on Beth's shoulders, gripping strongly. She pushed her hips into Beth, grinding in circles. Beth reached behind her and turned off the water. With an arm firmly around Mary's waist, she led her to the bed and lowered them both down, herself on top.

Mary's eyes were wild. Neither of them spoke at first, engrossed in a rapt kiss. When Mary reached up to pull Beth's soaking shirt off, Beth clutched her wrists and pinned them to the bed. Mary moaned deeply. There was no mistaking that Beth was exciting her.

Returning to her breasts, Beth alternated between the two as Mary gulped, "Yes."

She let go of Mary's wrists to cup each breast, lightly pinching the nipple that wasn't in her mouth. Mary writhed, running her hands through Beth's thick, wet hair. Beth sucked harder on a nipple and Mary gasped, "This is incredible."

Beads of water rolled off Beth's face and onto Mary's chest as the air from the open window raised goose bumps over the both of them. Mary shifted and Beth's mouth came off her breast. An attempt to roll Beth over was thwarted as Beth leveraged her body over Mary's.

"Just what do you think you're doing?"

Mary almost pleaded. "I want you under me."

"I wanted a few things the other night, but you kept me pinned to the wall, remember? It's my turn."

Mary groaned a luscious groan and closed her eyes as

Beth ravished kisses down her body. Her cheek grazed Mary's soft, curly pubic hair and she inhaled electrifying, womanly freshness. Parting Mary's thighs, she moved between them. As she looked up she noticed Mary watching her, smiling.

"Now, is *this* a date?" Mary taunted playfully.

Beth laughed. "Let's call it a gathering of two."

She lowered her mouth onto Mary, closing her eyes in complete pleasure as her tongue found unbelievably provocative, swollen lips. She found just the right movement. Mary seemed to love slow, languid circles. Her hips matched Beth's motion, passionate murmurings rolled from her mouth.

"Yes. Just like that. Please don't stop, Beth. Don't stop."

Sliding a hand under and up around Mary's thigh, Beth massaged the soft, silky flesh of her stomach. Shifting her position slightly, she spread the moist, responsive lips to gain better access to Mary's clit, which was already enlarged and distended. Beth moved her tongue deftly over and around the swollen shaft, causing shudders through Mary's body.

"Oh, God," Mary moaned, making Beth swirl inside.

The feeling of a woman in her mouth, juices flowing down her chin, was such a high Beth wished it could last days. Mary squirmed and Beth knew all too well that the sudden tenseness inside, the clutching at Beth's hair, the increase in ragged breathing, signaled that she was approaching orgasm. Rather than increasing her tempo, Beth slowed down.

For a moment, Mary stopped breathing. Then, from the back of her throat, she moaned, "What are you doing?"

"Making this last."

Mary raised her head again to stare down at her. "You're torturing me."

"What a way to go."

Mary dropped her head back against the pillow with a

thud. Smiling, Beth began a series of waves that brought Mary deliriously close to climax, then eased back down. Each surge was shorter than the last and each moan louder than the one before. Riding each swell as she brought Mary closer and closer, Beth knew she had total control.

"I know what insanity feels like." Mary's voice came in gulps as her hands frantically searched for something to hold on to.

Just as she balled her fists into the comforter, Beth eased two fingers inside her. When she finally allowed Mary to climax, she came in wave upon wave of shattering orgasm. It lasted an exquisite eternity as she bucked on Beth's mouth, crying out Beth's name. Strange pulling sensations moved across Beth's back and shoulders, but she was too engrossed in Mary's center to think about their origin. Mary's moans turned into screams as she released every last passionate fragment of her being. Beth rode with her, an arm wrapped around her thigh, keeping her from shooting through the headboard. She stayed inside her, feeling the throbbing squeeze of her muscles as Mary kept bucking against her.

The room became silent except for Mary's ragged breathing. "Come here." She groped for Beth.

Beth moved up until her face was snuggled against Mary's neck.

"My legs are paralyzed," Mary groaned.

Beth chuckled. "So I take it a quick ten K run is out?"

Mary pushed her playfully and then wrapped her arms around her. She rubbed Beth's back, making her wince.

"What...?" Mary reached around to inspect and found long, red scratch marks running from her ass to her shoulders. "Oh, God. Beth, I'm so sorry." Her hand went to her mouth. "I'm not known for leaving marks."

"Don't worry. I guess I deserved it."

"I'll go get some aloe vera." Mary hopped off the bed, and as she tried to walk, her legs wobbled. "You kicked my ass."

Beth surprised herself by answering, "And don't you forget it,"

Mary laughed and returned with the gel, straddling Beth's ass. "Don't you forget *this*."

Beth's eyes rolled into the back of her head as she felt Mary's other set of lips brush against her ass, distended from stimulation, dripping with wetness.

"I won't, I won't." Beth groveled. The next thing she felt was Mary's hands on her back, cool and slick from the aloe vera gel. She took a deep breath.

"This should help," Mary said. "And no revealing tank tops for a few days. I don't want Alder coming after me with a blunt knife."

"Somehow I doubt that she would. It's pretty hard to defend someone who has a shit-eating grin on her face."

Mary continued to rub. "Beth, I don't want this to sound clichéd, but you were incredible."

Beth rolled over so that Mary now straddled her stomach. "It was great."

Mary bent to her and they kissed slowly, dreamily.

CHAPTER FOURTEEN

Beth dreamt erratic, fragmented dreams. Swimming in a warm ocean, running through a thick and damp forest, bushes scraping her back. She awoke with Mary's arm draped over her stomach. Listening to her slow, even breathing, she suspected Mary's dreams weren't as Freudian as her own. According to Mary's bedside clock, it was a little after six thirty. The sheets were still slightly damp from a shower they'd taken in the middle of the night.

Beth replayed how Mary had made love to her. They'd tossed and tangled the bed linens until the bedroom looked like a combat zone. The memory of Mary's mouth on her neck, her breasts, and between her legs made her chest swim. Her unbridled passion had enabled Beth to let go completely, easing into incredibly erotic positions, opening up to Mary fully. She relived a moment when Mary had gone down on her. Close to coming, Beth had looked down to witness Mary's expression change from lustful smiling to steamy concentration. They had even laughed and teased in between the intensity of their sex, until Beth's climax shook them both.

Beth's thoughts turned toward the day. They were scheduled for a six-mile run. And then what? *What do two casual sex partners do once they get out of bed?* She looked over at Mary, who was still sleeping soundly, the comforter rising and falling slowly over her chest. An awkward sensation niggled at her. With serious lovers, next mornings were easy to navigate. It went unsaid that they would spend the day together and then the next night, and so on. Just like one did in a committed relationship.

This, with Mary, was far from that. They'd spent two nights together, only getting out of bed yesterday to eat, wash, and go on their run. Beth felt like she was in some kind of limbo, ignoring the world outside these four walls. She felt panicky inside and her mind raced to make sense of what the hell she was doing.

How do you end casual sex?

Casual sex. Closing her eyes, Beth sighed heavily. The past forty-eight hours hadn't felt casual to her. She touched her lips to Mary's warm forehead, kissing her awake, and told her that she'd come by later for their run. The clock ticked past seven. Mary murmured something about the damp sheets and Beth slipped out of bed.

❖

Alder was in the kitchen polishing a silver tea set when Beth returned. She didn't seem surprised to see her walk in the front door so early on a Saturday morning.

Scrutinizing the task in front of her, Alder said, "There's something very traditional about polishing silver. Reminds me of how calm my mother used to look when she'd sit at our family's old kitchen table and polish. Calms me, too."

Beth managed a smile and with a gentle pat on Alder's back as she passed on her way outside to the back porch. She sat on the top step, staring at the flowers, resting her head in her hands. She barely heard Alder's step behind her and jumped when she spoke.

"From the looks of you, last night was either really great or really horrible."

Beth squinted up toward the older woman, who held two mugs of coffee. She scooted over, making room on the step. "It was a little of both."

Alder sat next to her. "Was Mary not behaving herself?"

Beth took the mug she was offered. "Well, no, but that was the really great part of the evening."

Alder chuckled. "When did it get horrible?"

Beth looked out over the flowers, her jaw set tight. "It's just not me, Alder."

"What's not you?"

"I'm not some…feral female who runs around having casual sex. Mary is. I'm not."

"And that pisses you off?" Alder asked.

"Yes, it pisses me off. Mary's not my type. She's spontaneous and wild. I can't have that in my life. I should be looking for a more stable woman. I want someone who's grounded. I want a trusting, real relationship, like the one I had with Stephanie."

Alder spoke slowly as if trying to understand what she was saying as she said it. "The Stephanie who cheated on you?"

Beth clamped her mouth shut. How "real" was that relationship? "Like Stephanie but not Stephanie," she corrected. "And certainly not Mary."

"She was that bad, huh?" Alder looked astonished. "Both nights? Not even an improvement with practice?"

Beth felt a rush of heat whip her cheeks. "Mary was great. It's just that one minute I'm having this unbelievable time with her, and the next, I'm running away. I don't know what I should do. I feel like shit. It's been fantastic, but then," she paused, thinking, "everything got strange this morning. I couldn't think. I knew why I was with Mary, but I also didn't know why. I feel like I'm in a fog bank and I can see vague shapes, but everything's a blurred jumble."

"What do you want, Beth?" It was a simple question.

"I want a normal relationship."

"Normal," Alder echoed.

"I have a certain kind of woman in mind," Beth said truthfully. "And Mary's not it."

❖

Mary answered her door looking way too sexy. She was wearing boxer shorts and a tank top. Her hair was ruffled from sleep. She grinned sleepily and took Beth's hand as naturally as if they'd known each other a lifetime. She led her inside to sit on the couch.

"Mmm. I've been asleep since you left." Mary squeezed her eyes shut, rubbing them with both hands. "Tell the world to go away."

Beth tensed. This conversation was going to be difficult. "I can't. It's clamoring at the door."

"If it doesn't have some righteous coffee in hand, tell it to go the hell away." Mary stretched, then let her gaze rest on Beth's face. She looked more beautiful than ever. Her cheeks still had a faint trace or two of sheet lines, and Mary had never seen such sultry bedroom eyes. "How's your back?"

Beth blushed. "It's fine."

"I really am sorry." Mary shook her head. "But you were driving me crazy, and I needed something to hold on to."

But what I really want to do is tell you that I'm falling for you. Beth's soft kiss upon her forehead when she'd woken earlier had felt wonderfully loving. Mary hadn't wanted her to leave that morning, or the one before. And, more significantly, she realized she hadn't wanted Beth to leave at all.

"It's okay," Beth said.

"Last night was beautiful." Mary trembled inside. She needed to tell Beth what her heart was screaming. But she wasn't fully awake and she didn't want to blurt out some garbled cliché.

"Mary," Beth said, before she could get herself together. "I want you to know where I'm coming from."

Mary tilted her head, blinking.

"I don't think we should train together," Beth began. "I don't know what got into me. The time we've spent together has been great. Better than great. It's just that I'm not…I mean, I can't just fall into this. With you. Shit. What happened last night and the night before can't happen again. Please know that you are wonderful. But I can't do this. And I think our training together will just make it worse."

Mary tried to remain still. Beth didn't want this? "I'm not quite sure what you mean, Beth. You mean the sex?"

"Yes. I don't jump into things like this. You may be okay with it, but I'm not. Only three months ago, I was in a stable relationship, and now I'm having sex in an alley. It's not reasonable, you know?"

Mary's heart sank. "I don't have to agree with you, but I think I understand what you're saying."

"This is not what I want my life to be like."

"I didn't think that we were planning your life, Beth."

How can she be that calm? Beth wondered with frustration. Obviously it came with the wild, spur-of-the-moment lifestyle. And as much as she was feeling attracted to Mary, she didn't want to be her current spur-of-the-moment. She stood, feeling absolutely wretched. "I really like you, Mary, but I can't do this."

Mary stood slowly and then reached for her. With her warm hands on Beth's arms, she said, "I won't say I'm sorry for the alley. Or my bedroom. But I am sorry you feel that way."

"Being with you was incredible." Beth fought imminent tears. "I imagine that sounds like bullshit right now."

"It doesn't. I was right there feeling you when we made love."

Beth turned and walked to the door, looking back at Mary as she unlocked it. She opened her mouth but no words came. She lowered her head, glancing sadly at the running shoes lined up in the hallway, and then walked out.

Mary stared at the door, wishing it would open again with Beth walking back in. She reached up and massaged her forehead. *She doesn't want you. Let her go.*

Maybe it was for the best. She'd probably let herself get caught up in the excitement of being around a woman she couldn't seem to get enough of. Even though she'd sensed a reticence in Beth at first, she recognized a beautiful soul. And the more Beth held back her true spirit, the more Mary yearned to get closer to it. Beth wasn't naturally unfriendly or standoffish, as she'd first appeared. But she was scared, and Mary couldn't blame her. She knew how daunting it was to put oneself out there. She'd lived it for years. In her own life, spending time in bed with a woman didn't mean that she wanted to pursue anything with her afterward. Until Beth. And Beth had just told her they had no future.

Just when Mary was feeling quite the opposite.

A prickling sensation teased the back of her neck and she turned toward the living room and saw its origin. She walked over to the mantel and picked up the photograph of Gwen.

Touching the image, she smiled, remembering the cabin in which they'd spent two wonderful weeks. She trailed her finger across the glass, letting it come to rest over Gwen's heart.

"I love you," she whispered and carried the photograph to the cabinet by her kitchen telephone. Tenderly, she laid the memory inside the top drawer and then pushed it shut.

❖

A stab of despair twisted inside Beth.

She got her car and realized that she had nowhere to go. The pain of being cheated on by her ex was one thing, but this was just as bad. Mary had done nothing but treat her lovingly and with tremendous kindness. Walking away had left Beth with an empty well of dark, gloomy nothingness.

Driving aimlessly, she gravitated toward the wharf and found a parking spot close to Ghirardelli Square. She walked to the boats and piers close to Alioto's Restaurant. In a covered walkway, in the heart of the wharf commerce, she purchased some steaming hot clam chowder. It was served in a hollowed-out round sourdough loaf and she cradled it close as she walked around the dock, past the moored fishing boats to the pier beyond.

Finding an empty bench off the main drag, she sat on top of the backrest, her feet on the bench seat. She set the bowl in her lap and unwrapped a spoon and napkin from a cellophane envelope. The soup was fresh and creamy. It coated her throat with warmth but she had trouble enjoying the flavor. She looked out over the water in front of her, and the fishermen in the boats below, then up to the sky. Just under the blanket of fog, at least ten or twelve seagulls floated, wings open to the ever-present San Francisco breeze. They hovered aloft, hopeful for a handout.

Beth took a breath so deep she felt her shoulders rise and fall with the entire weight of her life. Eight days before, she'd rolled into town, weary-eyed and beaten after driving all night. She'd escaped three years of deception, and she would never tolerate such behavior from a partner again.

What was wrong with her? She'd enjoyed every minute with Mary. But Mary would never be someone she could have a committed lovership with. Mary was looking for an affair. Beth, even after all her disillusionment, was looking for a relationship.

A seagull swiftly swooped down, squawking loudly. Starting, Beth almost dropped her sourdough bowl as the gull alit on the pier railing in front of her. She flung the now empty bread bowl onto the ground and watched as the gull virtually attacked it. It knew that its time alone with the feast would be short-lived. In a moment, seven or eight of the breed would crash land almost on top of him, vying for the bowl, squawking and flapping at each other.

Beth lifted her eyes to the glistening ripples in the bay. She had done the right thing, breaking off the affair before things really got out of hand. *I'm not that person*, she asserted. *I don't just fuck in an alley and act all casual.* As soon as she went back to L.A., Mary would find someone else.

I can't be that cavalier about things. Shit!

"Casual sex isn't serious sex," she argued out loud to the seagulls.

CHAPTER FIFTEEN

The fire station was fairly quiet most of Tuesday. Mary sat on the rec room couch, hunched over the coffee table, flipping inattentively through a magazine. While she hadn't wished for anyone to be rescued from a burning building or need medical attention, she longed for back-to-back calls. Even a false report of smoke or a minor car accident would be welcome. Anything to keep her mind off Beth.

She was still confused over their last conversation. Things had seemed to be going fine and she was beginning to really like Beth.

She was the first person to come along since Gwen had died who made her want to slow down and feel more than just physical intimacy. Since moving to San Francisco, she'd told very few people about Gwen's death, sharing only the broadest details. She had protected herself by tucking that painful episode away in the hope that one day the anguish would finally evaporate. It never had.

But spending time with Beth had opened up that part of her she'd kept locked up. Sharing the story of Gwen's death had felt so natural, Mary knew she was talking with a woman who could mean something to her. Not since Gwen had she let herself feel deeper feelings; it had been too scary to try. There was no connection with the women she'd dated. But when she was with Beth, the fear of getting close just melted away and Mary wanted to reach out to her.

"Make some cookies, woman." Tucker, another firefighter/paramedic, clapped his hand on her back as he walked by.

"Make your own cookies, Tucker."

"I probably should. You never put enough chocolate chips in yours."

Tall and wiry, Tucker was her closest friend at the station. They'd gone into more blazes shoulder to shoulder than anyone else she worked with.

"So tell me what you're moping around for." He lay on the floor, flung his booted feet up onto the coffee table, and commenced a series of sit-ups.

"I just feel like shit, that's all."

"Shit as in 'I ate something bad' or shit as in 'I'm gonna bash the next person that asks me what's wrong'?" He puffed each time he sat up.

"I met someone that I really like. And she doesn't feel the same way."

"Who could not like you, Mary? You're indescribably delicious."

"Like you would know."

"No, but I have to listen to all the women that come by here looking for you. They don't give too many details, but those are some wanton and shameless looks on their faces."

The best thing about working for the fire department in the City by the Bay was that Mary could be out without having to deal with negative attitudes about her sexuality. Half the men were gay as well.

"You exaggerate, my friend." She leaned back on the couch. "This one's different. She's amazing. I love talking with her. I love being with her. I haven't felt this way in a long time. And she doesn't want anything to do with me now."

"What did you do to her?"

Mary laughed, knowing that he was kidding. But maybe she had done something. "I wish I knew."

"Have you told her she's different from the rest?"

"No. I was just starting to feel that way when she told me she didn't want to see me anymore. As a matter of fact, when she came over the last time, I was so happy to see her I knew it would be the right time to let her know."

"But you didn't get the chance?"

Mary shook her head.

"That's tough." He got up and sat on the edge of the couch next to her. He ruffled her hair. "She doesn't know what she's missing."

The station phone rang and they both remained where they were, knowing one of the rookies would run to answer it.

"Mary," a voice called from the kitchen. "Phone's for you."

She got up and reached for the wall-mounted extension. After a few minutes talking, she hung up and plopped back onto the couch. Tucker had finished his sit-ups and was in the middle of stretching. "Was that her?"

"No. That was Maria."

"And who's Maria?"

"Someone I met about a month ago. She wants to hook up."

"Maybe that'll get your mind off your unrequited love."

Mary closed the magazine. "I doubt it."

❖

The weather was cold and miserable, which was just fine since it was one of Beth's rest days. After leaving Mary's on Saturday, she'd run a six-mile loop, the same route Mary had taken her on. On Sunday she ran the route again, only in the opposite direction. Both runs were wretched endeavors, punctuated with thoughts of Mary's wit and her engaging laugh. At certain street corners, or as she ran past a bakery or office building, remnants of past conversations came streaming back and her feet began to feel heavy.

On those days, her efforts became arduous and loathsome, and she berated herself for choosing the same route. But she had less than a week left and it was easier to stick to the routes she already knew. At least, that's what she'd told herself.

On Monday and Tuesday, she ran east down Market Street to the San Francisco Bay and back. The change in route did nothing to quell her thoughts about Mary. The memory of how Mary tasted and the sensations she felt when Mary's incredible hands glided over her body dominated her thoughts.

With no run scheduled for today, she took a long, hot shower. That was the extent of her productive activity. She moped around the house for the rest of the afternoon, chatting with the Coop's residents as they came and went. She called Candace, hoping for reports of a flurry of incoming work that would give her an excuse to leave. But there had been no such news.

Keith had gotten sick of Beth sulking around the house for the last three days, so he'd slapped her on the knee and announced that they were going out dancing. She'd grudgingly gone upstairs to change her clothes, but by the time she descended the staircase, she was actually looking forward to getting her mind off Mary. A little alcohol and some sweaty dancing would do her good.

"Two beers," she said. "And then we're going home."

Ten minutes later they walked in a bar called the Lexington. One quick look around the dark-paneled establishment told her otherwise. It was filled with women enjoying the Wednesday night beer special.

"I assumed you'd take me to a men's bar," Beth said, pleasantly surprised.

"I'm feeling a little pudgy, so I didn't want to hold my gut in all night at a men's place. Besides, you and I can cut a rug anywhere, honey," Keith declared and took her hand, leading her to the bar.

The first beer went down well. It was cool and frothy and Beth laughed with Keith as he entertained the women around them with flamboyant stories of his life. She relaxed and felt a little lighter than she had since breaking it off with Mary. But she was sad inside, feeling the paradox of liking someone very much yet knowing she was completely wrong.

Just run the race and then get back to L.A.

"I gotta pee," Keith said. "Be right back."

Beth ordered her second beer and another apple martini for Keith. She'd been so preoccupied by his amusing chronicles that she hadn't even looked about the bar that much. She propped her back against the counter and sipped her beer. It was an intimate place and the women all seemed to know each other. A knot of women danced on a small parquet floor toward the back and a woman with a shaved head and multiple piercings DJ'd for them. As one song ended, a few women left the dance floor, creating an opening that caused Beth to stare and clutch her stomach.

Mary was toward the back, dancing with a beautiful Latina in tight, low-riding jeans and an alluring red tank top. Beth was transfixed and a sudden queasiness washed over her. Was this woman a friend or was she a date? When she reached up and draped her arms around Mary's neck, Beth had her answer. She cursed herself for her inability to look away. As she stared pathetically, she kept hoping Mary would yank away the arms or shake her head at the woman, refusing her advances.

And then it dawned on Beth. She was looking at the real Mary. The player. The vainly cavalier lothario who had swept her into the alley and fucked her. She felt humiliated and angry at herself. And she had to get out of there.

Keith finally exited the bar and rushed up to Beth who was pacing out front. "What's the matter? Are you feeling okay?"

No, I feel miserable and sick to my stomach. "Let's go, okay?"

"Tell me what's wrong." He obviously hadn't spotted Mary.

"I just really want to go. I can take a cab if you want to stay."

"Of course not. I'm hanging with you tonight." He threw his arm around her shoulder and turned her toward the street. "A giant fast food burger should clear things up. And if that doesn't, a mess of fries will."

Beth wished it were that easy.

Knocking on the door of the Coop, Mary felt confident and excited. She was also scared to death because she'd spent the last few days missing Beth to the point where she'd decided to share her true feelings. She'd let Beth walk out her door without letting her know that she was falling for her. For too long she'd convinced herself that she lived out loud, grabbing at life's experiences with intensely robust exuberance. But it had all been in compensation, to avoid the deeper feelings she kept locked away. And when it came down to conquering the vulnerability created by her feelings for Beth, she'd hesitated and failed. She had simply listened wordlessly as Beth gave her the brush-off.

Alder answered the door, letting Mary into the foyer.

"Is Beth here?"

"Yes, and I must say, your timing is impeccable."

"Why is that?"

"She's leaving."

"She's what?" Mary said, on her way up the stairs before Alder could answer. When she reached Beth's doorway, she demanded, "Why are you going home?"

Beth's head jolted up in surprise. "What are you doing here?"

"Why are you going home?" Mary repeated.

Beth returned to her packing, grabbing a T-shirt off the bed. "I came up here to get away from drama, not find more."

"What drama is that?"

Beth ignored Mary's question. Thursday had passed with nothing more than a solitary run to fill the day, and Friday morning had taken its merry time to arrive. And by the time it did, Beth had gone through three cups of coffee and the morning paper, with thoughts of Mary and the Latina woman surging relentlessly through her head. Mary was a jumble of push and pull, wanting her but not hesitating to want someone else. Well, at least she hadn't let it go too far.

Still, it hurt nonetheless. Her heart had swirled every time they were together. She'd fallen into Mary's tracking beam and it had sucked her into foolish, wanton desire. She'd tried to sleep last night but only managed to grow increasingly agitated until she knew what she had to do. With as little sleep as she was getting, the race would be a bust anyway. Her life was waiting for her in L.A. It was time for Beth to reclaim it.

Mary began to say something else, but Beth interrupted her. "Those things aren't going to happen to me anymore."

"What things, Beth? What are you talking about?"

"You. You fucked me, then you fucked someone else right after." Her hands began to shake.

Mary stepped inside covering the distance between them in three slow strides. "You told me you didn't want to see me anymore, Beth."

"I'm not interested in sex for sport."

"Sex for sport?"

Beth's chest tightened and she squeezed the T-shirt she was holding, shaking it for emphasis. "We had sex in an alley, Mary. It was impulsive and…outrageous. All I wanted to do was get away from the lunacy I left in L.A., and then I met you and everything went crazy."

"Crazy is bad?"

"Yes!" she yelled. "That's not who I am."

Mary reached for Beth, seeing the consternation in her face. More than anyone, she knew what that meant. No one had ever been able to get through to her all the time she'd felt that way after losing Gwen. Her heart broke as Beth backed away. Knowing Beth was repelled by her cut Mary deeply. *It's not about what you want,* she thought, *she doesn't want you. Leave her alone.*

Taking in a deep breath, she said, "I'm sorry for what you're feeling. That was never my intention. You're amazing and I love being around you."

Beth dropped the T-shirt into her bag. She looked up just as Mary reached out and gently touched her cheek. She lowered her eyes. *Please don't touch me. It makes it too hard to do what I have to do*. When she looked up again, their faces were so close, she could feel the softness of Mary's breath.

Quietly, Mary said, "And by the way, I didn't fuck her."

Beth looked down, clamping her eyes shut. She couldn't look at the woman she'd so easily and willingly fallen into bed with.

"Don't leave on my account, Beth. Run the race."

Beth heard her leave quietly and strained to hear the sound of the front door closing.

"That's not who I am," she repeated, this time horribly alone.

❖

"What's this?" Beth came downstairs later to a large pot roast on the table. The entire Coop household was readying dinner. Keith placed mashed potatoes on the table, licking his fingers, and then waved a hand. "This, my dear, is part of your rent money."

Balancing an armful of glasses, Gina headed for the table. "And anyone that springs for eats is welcome back anytime."

Alder drew close. "I saw Mary when she stopped by earlier." She paused and then asked, "Is this a pre-race dinner or is it still a going-away dinner?"

"Going away."

Alder nodded meaningfully.

Beth sat down with the rest, trying to muster some happiness though she felt far from happy. "Wow. This is really great."

"The Coop's gonna miss you." Maureen raised a glass. "Here's to a lifetime Coop resident."

The others raised their glasses and laughed as they clinked their salutations. The chatter picked up as everyone began filling their plates. Strangely, Beth felt like she was in the middle of some sort of unconventional *Waltons* TV show episode. The story seemed to be coming to a conclusion: Elizabeth was out of mischief and John-Boy had righted the wrong and everything was fine on the mountain.

Keith leaned in close to her. "You know why it's called the Coop, don't you?"

"Because it is said that if you stay here long enough, you eventually get laid."

"Well?" His eyes were sparkling, hopeful.

"The Coop's reputation remains intact."

Keith whooped. "Well, hot damn and pass the peas."

On the back porch after dinner, with glasses of wine, Beth sat with the Coop's residents and listened to music from the ratty speakers. The fog lumbered overhead in a gray-black expanse. The sounds of the bottles clinking against glasses seemed magnified. Beth thought it might be the fog cover bouncing noises around. Or maybe, just maybe, she perceived things much more clearly now.

The Coop was such a great place, she reflected. If she lived in the city, she was sure she'd visit quite a bit. For a moment she fantasized about what it would be like if she were to move up here. She might keep her business or maybe even start a new one. She could buy her own Victorian, something small and neat. She smiled, thinking how nice it would be to look out of her own bay window, mug of hot coffee in her hands, and watch the cool, dense fog lay its heavy blanket over the neighborhood. Then she wondered about Mary. Would she be coming down the stairs, rubbing her eyes and reaching simultaneously for a mug of coffee and Beth's waist?

Beth chuckled to herself. Of course not. That was not Mary.

It was undeniable that Mary had made her feel wanted

again, desirable and sexy. But Mary no more wanted a relationship than Beth wanted a fling. Though brief, their time together had been warm and important, so picturing her in the fantasy Victorian made Beth sad. Their short-lived connection was just never meant to pan out that way.

Still, her head was drastically contradicted by her heart. Was she deliberately fooling herself? She had done her best to dissuade her heart for fear of more hurt in the long run. So why was love starting to feel like a risk worth taking again?

Keith shook her shoulder. "Hello? Earth to Beth? Where'd you go, girl?"

I was just thinking about how much fun I've had here."

"Don't forget why you originally came," Alder said.

Keith piped in, "The race. You should run it, Beth. You've been training for the past two weeks so don't let that go to waste."

"We were all planning on being there to support you," Maureen said from an oversized beach chair.

"Yeah, don't ruin our Saturday morning." Keith raised his glass of wine. "We need an excuse to sit on the sidelines and have morning mimosas."

Beth did want to run. She just didn't want to run into Mary. But with about fifteen thousand people scheduled to be there, she supposed the chances were slim. She could run the race and come back and shower at the Coop before getting on the road.

Beth sighed loudly. "Okay. I don't want to refuse you your mimosas."

Everyone cheered and Keith hugged her.

"Another toast to our brief, but welcome roommate." He lifted his glass and met the others over the middle of the wooden, party-worn table.

Beth caught Alder watching her. The serene look on her

face made Beth feel like the older woman could read her mind. Laughing, she said, "No more toasts. I guess I have a race tomorrow and I've got to get up at the crack of jack."

Alder looked up to the night sky. Stars were beginning to make their appearance, twinkling their reassuring presence. "The fog's beginning to clear."

Chapter Sixteen

Beth arrived at the start line early. She wanted to take extra time to stretch her calf muscle. It hadn't bothered her much the past few days, but thirteen miles would tax her legs.

The race would start on the Embarcadero. As the runners gathered on the waterfront, milling about and warming up, Beth kept off to the side of the street. She didn't think she could cope with seeing Mary. The sidelines filled with race supporters holding to-go coffee cups and huddling against each other in the cool San Francisco breeze. The fog was abnormally thin and Beth could see the dim outline of the sun hovering just beyond the haze.

More runners arrived and the race officials began making announcements over a loudspeaker system, thanking sponsors and welcoming participants. Many of the runners were sponsored, raising money for various charities. Some of these were mentioned. Onlookers cheered and waved banners. Beth heard her name being called and spotted Alder and the rest of the Coop waving from the street curb. She jogged over and hugged everyone.

"Thanks for being here. It really means a lot."

"We wouldn't let you run without your posse rooting

for you," Keith said as he cradled his thermos. No doubt it contained orange juice with a little kick.

"We'll meet up with you at the finish line," Alder said.

Beth nodded. "You know where it is, don't you? Golden Gate Park, in the Rose Garden."

"We'll be there. Have a great race." Alder waved as the group made their way through the crowd.

"Bathroom stations," the announcer blared, "are next to each water station. And there is disabled access."

Beth bent down and wrapped her hands around her ankles, giving her hamstrings a much-needed stretch. She felt someone touch her back and jerked upright.

"Mary," was all she could get out. She looked incredible, in short blue running shorts and a white long-sleeve T-shirt.

"Hi, I'm glad you decided to run." Mary's eyes sparkled but her smile seemed reserved. "It's good to see you."

"It is," Beth had to admit.

"Has your training gone well?"

"Yes." Running without Mary for the past few days had been difficult emotionally, but Beth had driven herself hard as a way of escaping her chaotic thoughts.

"When are you leaving for L.A.?" Mary asked.

"Later today."

"Ah, life will get back to normal pretty soon, then."

"As normal as it'll ever be, I guess."

"Know that I'll miss you."

Beth felt her resistance begin to dissolve. She couldn't just ignore the woman who made her feel so alive. She put her hand to her breast. "I never expected to meet someone like you, Mary. I'll miss you, too."

The truth was as uncomplicated as it was real.

Mary smiled, and the silence that fell between them was comfortable. "I enjoyed every second with you."

"You made me feel some wonderful things." Beth laughed. "In some unusual places."

"Just one unusual place."

"Well, it was quite an experience. I didn't think I had it in me."

Mary paused before saying, "It was like you were a lone candle, sitting there dark and still. You just needed to be relit." She smiled. "The best part is, you let me hold the match."

They looked at each other and Mary chuckled. "I know that sounded pretty corny. What I mean is that it made me feel good to spend time with you. You let me in and I liked what I felt."

"Thank you."

Beth didn't know what else to say. Her body screamed at her to tell Mary that she wanted her, but her brain wouldn't allow the confession. Inviting Mary back into her world just wouldn't be logical when she was planning to be in L.A. by tomorrow. She surveyed the runners gathering around them, awaiting their signal. They were in the fifth wave, starting almost thirty seconds after the race leaders. She returned her attention to Mary, catching an odd look on her face.

As if to break the tension and drag them onto safe ground, Mary said, "They're predicting seventy degrees later. Perfect running weather."

Beth nodded. "Have a really good race."

She felt an ache in her heart when Mary's face washed over with sadness. Mary leaned in and kissed her cheek. Her lips lingered there for a long moment, as though she might whisper something in Beth's ear, but the words never came. She turned and walked away toward the back of the pack.

Beth didn't move. Bodies jostled around her. Officials marshaled. The hum of excitement rose. Everyone smoothed their bibs and checked that they were wearing the timing chips scanned earlier. People who didn't return these were not counted as race finishers and had to pay a fine. Somewhere ahead, a wave of runners left. Their feet blurred as Beth wiped her eyes. A woman next to her fidgeted urgently with her shoes and Beth realized their turn had come.

At the loud pop of the starting gun, the mass of runners began to move out, clicking their built-in stopwatches on. Roughly twenty seconds after the gun, Beth crossed the start line midway in the pack. She ran slower than her usual pace, following her plan so she could establish her own pace rather than try to keep up with anyone else. She wondered where Mary was. Probably well behind her. Beth had last seen her disappearing behind a group of runners a long way back. With their paces being pretty equal, she doubted Mary would catch up to her.

Supporters cheered as they made their way past the Ferry Building, heading for Fisherman's Wharf. Listening to the return shouts from the runners, Beth felt intensely alone. Everyone looked so happy and spirited, but all she felt was despair. From the first time she'd gone out to train with Mary, she'd looked forward to running the race with her. She had pictured them sprinting side by side and hugging as they finished together. She had wanted to share that triumphant moment with Mary and no one else.

As she placed one foot in front of the other, she imagined the measured rhythm of Mary's breathing and the sight of her shoes striking the ground. In her mind, they talked, whiling away the minutes that often passed so slowly during a run. She swung her gaze up toward the tall shaft of Coit Tower and imagined Mary making some silly, sexy remark about its shape.

But she had put an end to that. She couldn't just have

Mary as a friend without desiring her with everything she had. After only two weeks, she knew how hazardous it would be to give in to that desire. She couldn't set herself up for more heartbreak. It would destroy her.

Beth focused on the back of the runner immediately in front of her and tried to think about anything but Mary. Her mouth. Her beautiful body. The hands that caressed Beth to the edge of reason and beyond, until she lost all control and her brain refused to work. She had never felt so completely physical, so free of the shackles of reason and belief. In those moments, it had seemed that anything was possible.

Brain chemistry was affected by great sex, she reminded herself. And making love with Mary had been exquisite. *Making love?* The thought jarred. Hadn't it been just sex? Wasn't that what she'd set out to have—a hot encounter or two? Some recreation between the sheets just to prove that she could be with another woman, that she could still feel good?

Beth's throat closed and her breathing became uneven, disturbing the timing of her strides. They were running uphill. She looked around, stunned to find herself on the Golden Gate Bridge with the ocean glinting far below. Seagulls swooped overhead. The sun had come out and Beth could count the rivets gleaming in the steel girders above her. She passed time that way, keeping her pace steady and getting herself back into rhythm. They *had* made love, she thought rebelliously. No matter what her cool, rational mind insisted, she could not deny Mary's tender touches and passionate kisses. She would never forget the way Mary held her after she came, like Beth was the most precious creature in the world. Mary was kind and caring. Her consideration was unwavering when they were together. Being with her had felt so…stable.

A lone thought floated to the front of her consciousness.

Maybe Mary wasn't the player Beth thought she was. She dismissed the idea immediately. Damn it, she could talk herself into anything, and so far her judgment hadn't been impressive. She'd fooled herself that Stephanie was wonderful, too. Mary was Mary, and no matter what Beth tried to make herself believe, that wasn't going to change.

She just needed to finish the race and go home.

She forced herself to breathe deeply as she followed the constant stream flowing around Vista Point on the loop back over the bridge, heading in the other direction. Once they reached the Presidio, she slowed at a water station, realizing she hadn't been taking in enough fluid.

The volunteer made the handoff yelling, "You're looking good."

She had three more miles to run. Beth's legs felt heavy and she knew she was dehydrated. Of all the practices ingrained over her years as a runner, drinking was second nature. She took for granted that she knew when to supply her body with the water and electrolyte she needed on long runs. She should have grabbed an energy gel at the last station.

Beth made an effort to relax. Everything was going to be fine. She felt a little weak, that was all. She should have trained more intensely for longer so she could have used the past few days to taper back. Her muscles were tiring more quickly than she'd hoped, but there was no need to panic. It didn't matter if her time was a little slower, she was only running for herself.

She dropped her pace and fell back behind the cluster of runners she'd been leading. They were going downhill into Richmond, bunching a little on the straight stretch of road. Cheering supporters lined the route approaching the green haven of Golden Gate Park. Beth thought she saw Alder, but she wasn't sure. She waved anyway and swerved toward a water station, belatedly picking up the small energy booster she needed.

Minutes later, it happened instantly and without warning. Making the turn onto Fulton Street, she felt a sudden tightening, followed by a burning tear, and then she was falling. She buckled and collapsed, first smashing her knees on the rough, pebbled pavement and then coming down hard on the palms of her hands. The excruciating burn caused her lungs to seize into knots, forcing out short, painful gasps as she writhed on the ground. Both knees were bloody and she rolled onto her back, grimacing in pain.

The sun had appeared again, unexpectedly blinding her. She had to get up. She had to get out of the way of those coming up behind her. At once the sun disappeared, but she realized its absence was not about cloud cover but the silhouette of a woman blocking the glare.

"My hand." The woman bent over her.

Mary.

Beth barely heard the command. Strong fingers wrapped around hers and a hand scooped under her armpit. She was on her feet again, wobbling and blinking.

Avoiding the other runners, they got out of the street and Mary helped her sit on the curb. Her right knee was the bloodiest. A large gash flowed quite freely. Mary pulled off her bib and T-shirt, which she pressed to the wound.

Her fire training helped her to assess Beth's condition. Peering into her eyes, she asked, "Beth, where are you?"

"I'm certainly not sitting in Tahiti with a cocktail."

"I guess you didn't hit your head when you went down."

"No. My calf cramped, but this time, it ripped into me like I'd never felt before. It started to tighten on the bridge but I ignored it. I drank some more water on Twenty-seventh Street, and that should have helped, but when I turned the corner back there it just went." She reached below her knee and gave the muscle a poke. "The cramp is gone now."

A medic in official attire pulled up on his bicycle. He grabbed a small kit from a bag behind his seat and crouched next to them. After a quick check of Beth's pupils, he asked, "Let's see."

Mary removed her bloody T-shirt and sat with her arm around Beth as the medic cleaned and bandaged the injuries to both knees.

Runners continued to pass by.

"I've screwed up your race," Beth said.

"You didn't do anything of the sort."

The medic helped her to her feet. They thanked him and as he bicycled away, Beth gingerly bent one knee and then the other, testing them.

"Are you okay?" Mary asked. "Do you feel dizzy?"

Beth shook her head. "No. I'm fine, but I'm not going to push my luck. Go ahead. Finish your race."

Having Mary's arm around her for the past few minutes had been excruciating. Even now, Beth wanted more than anything to nestle her face into Mary's neck and just fall into her. But it was self-punishment to desire someone who only wanted an affair. Mary was the perfect woman in an imperfect situation.

"Tell me what the matter is, Beth. Do you need me to help you walk?"

The matter is that I wish you were interested in more than just playing around.

Beth suppressed a sob of exhaustion and defeat. Her bloodied legs were rapidly tightening up and she could barely move them. Her mind, her heart and her legs were wholly defeated.

"No. Really. I'll be fine."

"If you want to run without me, I can—"

"I can't do this, Mary," Beth shouted. "It's too hard. Please. Just go." *And stop breaking my heart!*

Mary flinched as if she'd been slapped. The look on her face pierced Beth's heart. Without another word, she stepped back, took a last long look at Beth, and jogged off.

Beth knew she needed to move but all she could do was stare after her, craning to see her as more runners filed past and her view got blocked. She could still see a blond head and Mary's race number, but only in glimpses. And then she was out of sight, mixed in with the rest of the mass, heading into the final miles.

Beth heart sank. What in God's name had she done? She'd fallen desperately for Mary and wanted nothing more than to tell her so, but Mary was gone for good. What more did she have to lose? She couldn't imagine her heart aching any more than it did right then, so it couldn't have done any more damage to tell Mary how she felt. She was undeniably and staggeringly in love with her. Instead she'd listened to her jumbled-up head and channeled all that desire into anger. Her mouth had shifted into high gear and she'd driven Mary away.

Wracked with anguish, she bent over. The pain in her legs intensified as the throbbing began to deepen. She closed her eyes against the horrifying image of Mary's parting expression. She'd lost her chance and screwed everything up.

If you would only come back, I could tell you how I really feel. Oh, my God. What have I done?

Mary had run less than a block when she slowed her pace. Something wasn't right. Beth had all but told her to go to hell, but her expression had communicated a different message. Mary had seen the same consternation on her face before. She'd seen it when Beth rebuffed her, at times when she seemed to feel vulnerable. Mary now knew what it meant. Beth wasn't rejecting her. She was trying to protect herself.

Her expression at those moments wasn't disinterest, but a longing for something she couldn't have. It was glaringly obvious that Beth was denying her true feelings. Mary understood her apprehension and had politely acquiesced. But in doing so, she suspected she'd sent Beth a message—that she wasn't interested enough to pursue her.

She'd been a coward, unwilling to own up to the feelings Beth aroused. The depth of her attraction disturbed her. She found herself dealing with a sharp sense of loss every time she walked away from Beth. The feeling pushed her buttons.

Beth was recovering from a breakup. Women in her situation found consolation in someone's arms. They had affairs that didn't last. Mary understood that, firsthand, and that experience had made her uneasy. She didn't want to be discarded when Beth was ready to move on. But was she going to squelch a chance for love because she feared she would be left alone again?

Mary slowed down and looked back. She couldn't see Beth. And by tomorrow, she knew Beth would be gone. The thought felt like a kick to the heart.

Blood dripped from Beth's bandage. She'd traveled all this way and had come up short of the finish line. Worse, she'd come up short in a love that was new and unexpected. Holding back a torrent of tears, she watched the runners pouring into Golden Gate Park. There would be buses shuttling participants back to the staging area at Justin Herman Plaza. If she took her time, she could make her way to the finish line and find transport.

A rumble of voices caught her attention. She couldn't tell what the spectators around her were saying, but quite a few people were craning to see something down the road. The faces of the crowd were all fixed in the same direction.

Through the cluster of race entrants running toward the park, a lone woman ran in the opposite direction. The runners were parting left and right to stream around her, allowing Beth a clear view. Her heart swelled. Mary, with a determined look on her face, was headed straight for her. *She's coming back for me.*

Beth stepped out into the street. The buzz of the spectators' curiosity increased, but it was white noise to Beth. She was transfixed by the woman running her way. Mary's strong legs flexed and her hair bobbed up and down with her strides. She was magnificent.

Beth had tried to drive her away, knowing that someone like her would have her fun and then leave anyway. But she knew now that she'd been terribly wrong. As much as she couldn't get Mary out of her heart, Mary wouldn't be driven away.

Run to me, Beth thought, then took to her feet, running straight for Mary with no regard to pain or the startled gasps of the crowd. Immediately they were in each other's arms, heads tucked into each other's necks, embracing tightly.

"I can't leave you," Mary declared. "I am crazy about you. I needed to tell you but I didn't think you wanted me."

"I want you, Mary. I'm so sorry for yelling at you." Beth held on even tighter. "I've been afraid to love you."

Mary pulled back until they could look into each other's eyes. "Why?"

"You don't want to settle down. And I'm the settle-down type."

Mary took a deep breath. "Gwen's death has had me in a stranglehold for too long. I held on to that love long after I should have. But when you and I made love, that changed."

"But what about the other women?"

"My idiotic way of compensating. Until I met you, I never wanted to get really close to anyone in that way. You've changed that, Beth. My God, you've changed everything. I want to love you. Only you."

Beth tilted her head, peering into Mary's eyes, finally letting herself see the woman Mary was, not the player she'd gauged her to be. She was right there, tenderly regarding Beth, a hand cupped to her cheek, eyes bright with emotion.

"I've been a fool," Beth said.

Mary's growing affection for her had not been a farce. Mary wanted her. *She ran to me, even after I yelled at her to go.* With that realization, Beth allowed into her heart all the possibilities that loving Mary could offer. She made Beth feel appreciated and desired. With her, Beth knew a joy she hadn't thought was possible.

"We've both been dancing around this," Mary said. "Resisting the inevitable."

Beth grinned. "The inevitable. Is that another law of thermodynamics?"

"For us, yes. There are times when you just can't put out a fire."

"I tried," Beth conceded. "I've been fighting all these emotions. And because I thought you only wanted a casual affair, I was trying to hide my feelings. And this desire…this incredible desire."

Mary stroked Beth's cheek. "Don't ever hide that part of you."

"Somehow I don't think I'll be able to now."

"Your love is so amazing. It's beautiful when you let it out." Mary kissed her briefly and softly. "And I'm going to let it all out, too."

"I love you, Mary."

Mary's voice shook. "And I love you."

"Let's finish what we started." Beth looked up and down the street.

Thin streams of runners passed by, petering out as the final wave left Beth and Mary standing out in the road, alone. The spectators and officials had already started off toward the finish line, eager to be there for the closing.

"Oh, yes," Mary said. "First we need to get you a ride to the finish line."

"But we're going to finish what we started, and the race is the first step."

"You're in no condition to run."

"If you'll help me, I can do this. After all, you did come back for me."

"I'm sorry I left in the first place."

Beth put her arms around Mary's neck. "All that matter is that you're here."

They kissed briefly but tenderly, then turned toward the park and began to run together. The few people that were still around them enthusiastically clapped.

"How are your knees?" Mary asked after a few strides.

"They hurt like hell." As a matter of fact, the pain was severe, but Beth would endure anything as long as Mary was next to her.

"Let's just go slowly. But tell me if you need to stop."

As they progressed through the park, each footfall was torture. "There's no stopping now."

"The race or us?"

"Both." Beth stumbled, and Mary grabbed her around the waist.

"We need to stop." Mary's voice was full of concern.

"No, let's do this."

Starting now, Beth promised herself, she was not looking back. She'd almost lost a chance at love, and maybe she would make a few mistakes with Mary, but none of them would be about running away.

The finish line stood only a hundred yards ahead. Beth could see the Coop residents yelling and waving at them. Mary held on to her and they slowly approached the end of the race. A concerned look materialized on Alder's face when she noticed the bloodied knees. Beth gave her friends a thumbs-up and heard Alder's booming voice.

"Regrets be damned!"

After ten more strides, Beth and Mary crossed the finish line together.

Many hours later, in a sea of blankets and rumpled sheets, they held each other. Early morning light filtered in from the tiny window in Beth's attic room. Their race clothes were in a small pile by the door and two towels from their shower hung over the bathroom door.

"You missed your departure to L.A." Mary traced her fingers lightly across Beth's breasts.

"Looks like it." Beth's voice was low. "You know what one of the greatest things was, yesterday?"

"Finishing the race?"

Beth shook her head. "Feeling you come in my mouth last night."

Mary's eyes flew open. "Yeah?"

"Yeah. I felt your muscles contracting. Right here." Beth touched a finger to her chin.

Mary raised her hand. "Waiter. Check, please!"

"And what you did later on was amazing, too."

"I afraid you'll have to be more specific."

Beth rolled Mary onto her stomach and positioned herself over her. "Let me show you."

Mary knew what she was referring to. With a lusty groan of anticipation, she dropped her face into the pillow as Beth lowered her naked body. Beth's public bone pressed down on her ass and slowly began to grind into her. As she did so, Mary grabbed handfuls of the bottom sheet with her fists to anchor them both. Tightening her ass muscles, she pushed up to meet each thrust. She could feel Beth adjusting, finding just the right spot. When her clit was right where she wanted it, Mary felt her quiver. And when Beth reached over and held Mary by her wrists, restraining her, Mary's clit began to throb.

They moved together, Beth pushing against her from behind. Mary's head spun as the movements increased. She could feel Beth's breasts sliding up and down against her back. She wanted to reach down and touch herself, but it excited her that much more to be pinned down.

Beth's ragged voice was hot on her neck. "I can't believe I'm going to come this way."

"Take your time, baby," Mary encouraged.

Beth began to tremble and her thrusts quickened rhythmically. "I can't," was all she said and then her breathing grew stronger and she bucked against Mary, calling out her name. She continued to grind into her, calling out, "Yes, baby," while Mary pushed up against her.

As the trembling subsided, Mary felt Beth's weight come to rest on her. She turned over, pulling Beth down on top of her. They lay there, arms wrapped around one another.

"I loved that," Mary said.

"I've never done that before." Beth nibbled Mary's ear.

"I believe there will be a lot of new things for you and me," Mary said.

. Beth drew in a deep, contented breath. She finally understood why she had really escaped L.A. She'd lost herself in a relationship that was wrong for her, and yet she couldn't see that clearly. Her idea of the right woman had been a fabricated image of what she thought she wanted. She'd felt like a failure when she couldn't mold her life to fit the fantasy.

Then, right in front of her, appeared a wonderful woman she wanted more than she'd ever wanted anyone. But Mary didn't fit her preconceived notions. Beth smiled. She was more than happy to discard her old ideas for new ones that suited her better. She'd driven out of L.A. to lose herself. It was quite a shock to realize that here, in the middle of the city of fog, she had actually found herself instead.

She cupped her hand around Mary's face. "I almost lost you."

"And I almost let you get away," Mary said, and just before they kissed again, she added, "So we're even."

About the Author

Lisa Girolami has been in the entertainment industry since 1979. She holds a BA in Fine Art and an MS in Psychology. Previous jobs included ten years as a production executive in the motion picture industry and another two decades producing and designing theme parks for Disney and Universal Studios. She is also a counselor at a mental health facility in Garden Grove.

Writing has been a passion for her since she wrote and illustrated her first comic books at the restless age of six. Her imagination usually gets the best of her, and plotting her next novel during boring corporate meetings keeps her from going stir-crazy. She currently lives in Long Beach, California.

Visit her online at www.LisaGirolami.com.

Books Available From Bold Strokes Books

truelesbianlove.com by Carsen Taite. Mackenzie Lewis and Dr. Jordan Wagner have very different ideas about love, but discover truelesbianlove is closer than a click away. (978-1-60282-071-5)

Justice at Risk by John Morgan Wilson. Benjamin Justice's blind date leads to a rare opportunity for legitimate work, but a reckless risk changes his life forever. (978-1-60282-059-3)

Run to Me by Lisa Girolami. Burned by the four-letter word called love, the only thing Beth Standish wants to do is run for—or maybe from—her life. (978-1-60282-034-0)

Split the Aces by Jove Belle. In the neon glare of Sin City, two women ride a wave of passion that threatens to consume them in a world of fast money and fast times. (978-1-60282-033-3)

Uncharted Passage by Julie Cannon. Two women on a vacation that turns deadly face down one of nature's most ruthless killers—and find themselves falling in love. (978-1-60282-032-6)

Night Call by Radclyffe. All medevac helicopter pilot Jett McNally wants to do is fly and forget about the horror and heartbreak she left behind in the Middle East, but anesthesiologist Tristan Holmes has other plans. (978-1-60282-031-9)

Lake Effect Snow by C.P. Rowlands. News correspondent Annie T. Booker and FBI Agent Sarah Moore struggle to stay one step ahead of disaster as Annie's life becomes the war zone she once reported on. Eclipse EBook (978-1-60282-068-5)

Revision of Justice by John Morgan Wilson. Murder shifts into high gear, propelling Benjamin Justice into a raging fire that consumes the Hollywood Hills, burning steadily toward the famous Hollywood Sign—and the identity of a cold-blooded killer. Gay Mystery. (978-1-60282-058-6)

I Dare You by Larkin Rose. Stripper by night, corporate raider by day, Kelsey's only looking for sex and power, until she meets a woman who stirs her heart and her body. (978-1-60282-030-2)

Truth Behind the Mask by Lesley Davis. Erith Baylor is drawn to Sentinel Pagan Osborne's quiet strength, but the secrets between them strain duty and family ties. (978-1-60282-029-6)

Cooper's Deale by KI Thompson. Two would-be lovers and a decidedly inopportune murder spell trouble for Addy Cooper, no matter which way the cards fall. (978-1-60282-028-9)

Romantic Interludes 1: Discovery ed. by Radclyffe and Stacia Seaman. An anthology of sensual, erotic contemporary love stories from the best-selling Bold Strokes authors. (978-1-60282-027-2)

A Guarded Heart by Jennifer Fulton. The last place FBI Special Agent Pat Roussel expects to find herself is assigned to an illicit private security gig baby-sitting a celebrity. (Ebook) (978-1-60282-067-8)

Saving Grace by Jennifer Fulton. Champion swimmer Dawn Beaumont, injured in a car crash she caused, flees to Moon Island, where scientist Grace Ramsay welcomes her. (Ebook) (978-1-60282-066-1)

The Sacred Shore by Jennifer Fulton. Successful tech industry survivor Merris Randall does not believe in love at first sight until she meets Olivia Pearce. (Ebook) (978-1-60282-065-4)

Passion Bay by Jennifer Fulton. Two women from different ends of the earth meet in paradise. Author's expanded edition. (Ebook) (978-1-60282-064-7)

Never Wake by Gabrielle Goldsby. After a brutal attack, Emma Webster becomes a self-sentenced prisoner inside her condo—until the world outside her window goes silent. (Ebook) (978-1-60282-063-0)

The Caretaker's Daughter by Gabrielle Goldsby. Against the backdrop of a nineteenth-century English country estate, two women struggle to find love. (Ebook) (978-1-60282-062-3)

Simple Justice by John Morgan Wilson. When a pretty-boy cokehead is murdered, former LA reporter Benjamin Justice and his reluctant new partner, Alexandra Templeton, must unveil the real killer. (978-1-60282-057-9)

Remember Tomorrow by Gabrielle Goldsby. Cees Bannigan and Arieanna Simon find that a successful relationship rests in remembering the mistakes of the past. (978-1-60282-026-5)

Put Away Wet by Susan Smith. Jocelyn "Joey" Fellows has just been savagely dumped—when she posts an online personal ad, she discovers more than just the great sex she expected. (978-1-60282-025-8)

Homecoming by Nell Stark. Sarah Storm loses everything that matters—family, future dreams, and love—will her new "straight" roommate cause Sarah to take a chance at happiness? (978-1-60282-024-1)

The Three by Meghan O'Brien. A daring, provocative exploration of love and sexuality. Two lovers, Elin and Kael, struggle to survive in a postapocalyptic world. (Ebook) (978-1-60282-056-2)

Falling Star by Gill McKnight. Solley Rayner hopes a few weeks with her family will help heal her shattered dreams, but she hasn't counted on meeting a woman who stirs her heart. (978-1-60282-023-4)

Lethal Affairs by Kim Baldwin and Xenia Alexiou. Elite operative Domino is no stranger to peril, but her investigation of journalist Hayley Ward will test more than her skills. (978-1-60282-022-7)

A Place to Rest by Erin Dutton. Sawyer Drake doesn't know what she wants from life until she meets Jori Diamantina—only trouble is, Jori doesn't seem to share her desire. (978-1-60282-021-0)

Warrior's Valor by Gun Brooke. Dwyn Izsontro and Emeron D'Artansis must put aside personal animosity and unwelcome attraction to defeat an enemy of the Protector of the Realm. (978-1-60282-020-3)

Finding Home by Georgia Beers. Take two polar-opposite women with an attraction for one another they're trying desperately to ignore, throw in a far-too-observant dog, and then sit back and enjoy the romance. (978-1-60282-019-7)

Word of Honor by Radclyffe. All Secret Service Agent Cameron Roberts and First Daughter Blair Powell want is a small intimate wedding, but the paparazzi and a domestic terrorist have other plans. (978-1-60282-018-0)

Hotel Liaison by JLee Meyer. Two women searching through a secret past discover that their brief hotel liaison is only the beginning. Will they risk their careers—and their hearts—to follow through on their desires? (978-1-60282-017-3)

Love on Location by Lisa Girolami. Hollywood film producer Kate Nyland and artist Dawn Brock discover that love doesn't always follow the script. (978-1-60282-016-6)

Edge of Darkness by Jove Belle. Investigator Diana Collins charges at life with an irreverent comment and a right hook, but even those may not protect her heart from a charming villain. (978-1-60282-015-9)

Thirteen Hours by Meghan O'Brien. Workaholic Dana Watts's life takes a sudden turn when an unexpected interruption arrives in the form of the most beautiful breasts she has ever seen—stripper Laurel Stanley's. (978-1-60282-014-2)

In Deep Waters 2 by Radclyffe and Karin Kallmaker. All bets are off when two award winning-authors deal the cards of love and passion… and every hand is a winner. (978-1-60282-013-5)

Pink by Jennifer Harris. An irrepressible heroine frolics, frets, and navigates through the "what ifs" of her life: all the unexpected turns of fortune, fame, and karma. (978-1-60282-043-2)

Deal with the Devil by Ali Vali. New Orleans crime boss Cain Casey brings her fury down on the men who threatened her family, and blood and bullets fly. (978-1-60282-012-8)

Naked Heart by Jennifer Fulton. When a sexy ex-CIA agent sets out to seduce and entrap a powerful CEO, there's more to this plan than meets the eye…or the flogger. (978-1-60282-011-1)

Heart of the Matter by KI Thompson. TV newscaster Kate Foster is Professor Ellen Webster's dream girl, but Kate doesn't know Ellen exists…until an accident changes everything. (978-1-60282-010-4)

Heartland by Julie Cannon. When political strategist Rachel Stanton and dude ranch owner Shivley McCoy collide on an empty country road, fate intervenes. (978-1-60282-009-8)

Shadow of the Knife by Jane Fletcher. Militia Rookie Ellen Mittal has no idea just how complex and dangerous her life is about to become. A Celaeno series adventure romance. (978-1-60282-008-1)

To Protect and Serve by VK Powell. Lieutenant Alex Troy is caught in the paradox of her life—to hold steadfast to her professional oath or to protect the woman she loves. (978-1-60282-007-4)

Deeper by Ronica Black. Former homicide detective Erin McKenzie and her fiancée Elizabeth Adams couldn't be happier—until the not-so-distant past comes knocking at the door. (978-1-60282-006-7)

The Lonely Hearts Club by Radclyffe. Take three friends, add two ex-lovers and several new ones, and the result is a recipe for explosive rivalries and incendiary romance. (978-1-60282-005-0)

Venus Besieged by Andrews & Austin. Teague Richfield heads for Sedona and the sensual arms of psychic astrologer Callie Rivers for a much-needed romantic reunion. (978-1-60282-004-3)

Branded Ann by Merry Shannon. Pirate Branded Ann raids a merchant vessel to obtain a treasure map and gets more than she bargained for with the widow Violet. (978-1-60282-003-6)

American Goth by JD Glass. Trapped by an unsuspected inheritance and guided only by the guardian who holds the secret to her future, Samantha Cray fights to fulfill her destiny. (978-1-60282-002-9)

Learning Curve by Rachel Spangler. Ashton Clarke is perfectly content with her life until she meets the intriguing Professor Carrie Fletcher, who isn't looking for a relationship with anyone. (978-1-60282-001-2)

Place of Exile by Rose Beecham. Sheriff's detective Jude Devine struggles with ghosts of her past and an ex-lover who still haunts her dreams. (978-1-933110-98-1)

Fully Involved by Erin Dutton. A love that has smoldered for years ignites when two women and one little boy come together in the aftermath of tragedy. (978-1-933110-99-8)

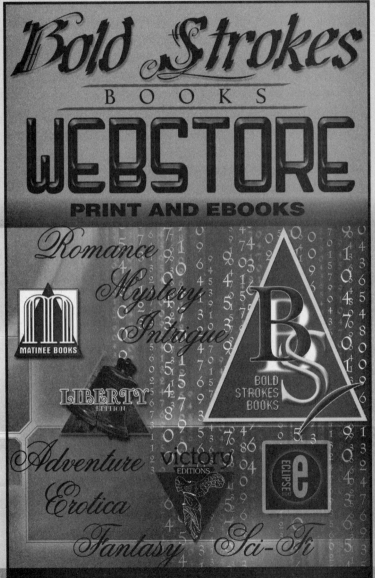